BEAUTIFUL STEPBROTHER

STONI ALEXANDER

SILVERSTONE PUBLISHING

Edited by Nicole, Proof Before You Publish
Proofread by Carole, Too Thorough for Words
Cover design by Johnny & Stoni; Photo by Shutterstock

Published in the U.S. by SilverStone Publishing, 2019
ISBN 978-1-946534-06-4 (Print Paperback)
ISBN 978-1-946534-07-1 (Kindle eBook)

To the beautiful bloggers who share my love stories.
Your support means so much to me!

ABOUT BEAUTIFUL STEPBROTHER

Look, but don't touch...

Thriving land developer Zander King lives to work and works to win. He's tightly wound, in complete control, and by the book. That makes him a great CEO...at a cost.

He could have his pick of the many beautiful women who throw themselves at him. But there's no room in his life for a girlfriend, let alone love. For him, relationships are physical and fleeting.

That is, until a shared tragedy reunites him with landscape photographer Savannah Morrissette. She's different. Gorgeous? *Check.* Sexy? *Check.* But she's got a sassy edge to her super laid-back vibe. *And that makes her so damned irresistible.*

When Zander learns Savannah is blocking the biggest deal of his career, he's determined to make her see things his way. But she's no pushover. He must find a way to work with her as their attraction—and temptation—escalate to a feverish pitch.

They say mixing business with pleasure is never a good idea. But how can it be wrong if it feels so right?

ZANDER KING

Nothing like a midday fuck.

Breathing hard, Zander King rolled onto his back. He closed his eyes and relaxed against the soft mattress. His taut back muscles released and the last remaining angst faded away. His companion propped up on an elbow.

"I got offered the job in Nashville," she said.

His phone rang on her night table and he silenced it. *Not yet.* Work could wait five more minutes. He needed to cling to the sex high for as long as he could.

"Congrats." He would miss her perks more than he'd miss her. "When do you leave?"

"About a week. Nothing holding me here." The longing in her eyes didn't jibe with her words. But he couldn't ask her to stay.

Two weeks ago, they'd been introduced through mutual friends at a business event. He hadn't been interested enough to pursue her, but she called. Zander explained he had zero work-life balance and didn't have time to get involved. She persisted. They'd gone out, had sex. A week later, she called again. They'd done more of the same. When she invited him to drop by for a quickie, he decided it would be his last.

Turns out, the universe agreed.

"The company is lucky to have you." Zander dropped a quick peck on her forehead before pushing out of bed. Drawn-out goodbyes weren't his thing. He closed the bathroom door, removed the condom, and cleaned off. When he returned to the bedroom to get dressed, she was gone, and the bed had been made. He found her making a sandwich in her cramped kitchen.

"Once I'm settled, maybe you'll visit me." She shoved the sleeves of her sweatshirt up her forearms.

Not happening. "I don't have any projects in Tennessee and I don't see myself getting away anytime soon. I'm sorry. Good luck in your new job." He shut the front door of her townhouse without glancing back. Though he was confident she was spewing profanities, he wouldn't make an empty promise. His life had been filled with those. No way in hell would he pay that forward.

Outside, the afternoon humidity engulfed him. Early September in the D.C. region offered no reprieve from the sweltering, sticky heat. On the way to his car, he scrolled through his phone. Seven missed calls. No new texts. He re-read the previous day's text from his father.

"I love you, son."

"Love you, too, Dad," he'd texted back, surprised to have heard from his old man at all.

Zander couldn't recall the last time his dad had said those words. Ever since leaving for college, seventeen years ago, Zander had initiated every phone call, every text, and every visit.

Until yesterday.

After slipping inside his Porsche, he started it up and blasted the air. Before cutting into traffic, he punched up his voice messages.

"Hey, Zander, I've got an update on Starry Cove." Kent Walker, Senior Vice President of King Development. "See me when you get back."

Zander couldn't miss the tightness in his business partner's voice. *Dammit, that can't be good. Too many problems at work. When am I gonna get a break?*

Message playback continued. "Hey, Zander baby, let's get together sometime for dinner," said a woman whose voice he didn't recognize. "Text me when you're free."

At a red light, he continued listening.

"Mr. King, this is Sheldon Elstor. Please call me back as soon as possible. I have an urgent matter to discuss with you." The stranger rattled off his phone number and hung up. *What does he want?*

The messages droned on. "Zander, it's Stu. Great presentation. Unfortunately, we're going with a different developer. Appreciate your efforts." *Ah, hell. We needed that deal.*

Another message from Kent. "It's me again. Esteem is thirty days overdue on their first payment toward the hundred and twenty-five mil they owe us. Without it, we might default on our loan. On top of that, the CFO isn't returning my calls. My blood pressure is through the roof."

In the last few months, Zander's company had hit a rough patch. His two biggest projects, Starry Cove and Esteem University, were derailing. While he couldn't get the Starry Cove deal off the ground because a landowner objected to his proposal, Esteem University was well underway. The successful online university boasted a global student body of nearly one hundred thousand and was eager to build a brick and mortar campus nestled in the thriving Chantilly, Virginia area. King Development had financed the project's start by providing one hundred and twenty-five million of borrowed funds toward developing the six-building campus.

In addition to these problems, Zander hadn't won as much new business as he'd forecasted. These setbacks meant income delays, but the loans still had to be paid monthly. He rubbed his forehead, hoping to ward off another stress headache. *If things don't improve, I might have to file for bankruptcy.*

The light changed, but the pickup in front of him didn't budge. Northern Virginia traffic gridlocked without the assistance of a stopped vehicle in the middle of the road. The driver behind him laid on his horn.

An attractive, tanned woman wearing a white tank, ripped jeans, and sandals emerged from the truck, yanked jumper cables from the bed, and marched toward the engine.

A car whizzed by, almost clipping her. Zander punched on his flashers, jumped out, and strode over. "Want me to push you off the road?"

Intense eyes flashed in his direction, but a chunk of mussed hair draped her brows, casting the rest of her face in shadow. She raised the hood. "I need a jump."

Beyond her rich, sultry voice, he was struck by an odd feeling of déjà vu. "Do I know you?"

"Doubtful. I don't live around here." She nodded toward his car. "Can I plug into you?"

"I'll pull up." He dragged his attention from her pretty face and eyed her truck. Jalopy had to be twenty-five years old. Traffic sped by. "Slow the hell down," he shouted as he headed back to his car.

The blazing September sun, coupled with the thick, humid air, had him wiping perspiration from his brow. He removed his suit jacket and rolled up his sleeves. After pulling onto the shoulder and up alongside her, he popped his hood and removed the battery cover.

While she clamped her cables to his battery, he checked her out. No doubt the woman was hot and, if the circumstances had been different, he might have shown more interest.

Her phone blared and she fished it out of her back pocket. "Hey," she answered. "Hello, are you there?" She stared at her phone. "Crap. My battery died."

When she climbed into her vehicle, Zander followed. Leaning

over, she checked inside her glove box, then rummaged under a pile of photographs on the passenger seat.

He flicked his gaze to her curvy ass. "Can you start your engine, please? I've got to get back to work."

Ignoring him, she dumped out the contents of her giant bag and mumbled, "Sons o' bitches. Where's that charger?"

His lips twitched. Clearly, she wasn't big on technology. He had backup chargers in his vehicles, his home, and his office. He glimpsed her cell phone. Doubtful his charger would work on her outdated flip phone.

Beads of sweat trickled down Zander's back. "*Excuse me.*" She stopped searching and pinned him with a frosty stare. "It might help if you start your truck."

"Oh, right." She turned the key. "I really needed to take that call." After a few chokes and sputters, her vehicle roared to life.

With his good deed completed, Zander was ready to take off. "Can you remove the cables so I can roll?"

As soon as she did, the engine died. "Truck's been having trouble staying juiced." The brunette re-clamped the cables and started her vehicle. "It'll be fine in a couple of minutes. Can I borrow your phone while we wait?"

"It's too hot outside. I'm getting in my car. You can use my phone there."

"I don't get into cars with strangers, but where you gonna go? We're connected to each other." Her light-hearted laugh reminded him of his childhood. Something he hadn't thought about in years.

She slipped into the passenger seat and sighed. "Cold air feels great."

He glanced at the screen as he handed her his phone. Two missed calls and a text from Kent in the past five minutes.

She dug out a torn piece of paper from her back pocket and dialed the number jotted down. "He might not answer if he doesn't recognize the number."

"Text him—"

"It's Savannah," she said into the phone. "How's he doing?"

As she listened, he studied her profile. Dark, wavy hair framed her face. Every time she blinked, her bangs fluttered against her eyelashes. She had a sharp nose and full lips that bowed in the middle. Her tight tank hugged her breasts. But her beautiful face and curvy body weren't his priority at the moment. He wanted her clunker to hold a charge. *Time is money.*

Tears spilled from her eyes, and she brushed them from her cheeks. "I'm sorry I couldn't make it in time. I'm on a borrowed phone. I'll call you back once I find my charger. Later." When she hung up, another tear rolled down her cheek.

"You okay?" he asked.

"It's tough losing family. Life is short, you know?"

Though he wanted to comfort her, touching her would be inappropriate. Instead, he settled for, "I'm sorry for your loss."

"Thanks. He was a good guy."

Rap, rap, rap. A policewoman peered into his window. *Great. Now this.* Zander lowered his window.

"What's going on here?" asked the cop, while a second set up a flare.

"This woman's truck wouldn't start and I stopped to help." Zander gave the officer his driver's license.

She eyed his ID, handed it back. "The vehicle is running now. Can you continue your conversation elsewhere?"

He and Savannah exited his car. She unclamped the cables, threw them into her pickup, and thrust a twenty at him.

"Keep that." Zander flipped open his wallet and pulled out a slew of twenties. "Get yourself a new battery for your truck *and* your phone."

Her lips curved while her gaze floated over his face. "I can't take your money." Hopping into her vehicle, she eyed him through the rolled down passenger window. "Thanks for the jump, Slick."

As Savannah drove away, Zander secured the battery cover

and closed his hood. Soaked with perspiration, he slid behind the wheel and headed for his office.

Despite spying his cell phone on the passenger seat, he left it there. There was something about her loss that left him feeling blue. He envied her that she had family she cared about.

Zander's parents had split when he was five. He had murky memories of his mom. She used to run a long phone cord outside so she could smoke while she talked. Every time he'd join her, she'd whisper that she wasn't alone. Clearly, she didn't want him around. The day he learned his mother wasn't coming home was the last time he'd displayed any real emotion.

His father had found him sobbing on his bed. "You'll get over it, kid. Starting tomorrow, no tears. I don't need a crybaby for a son." When his father left the room, a loneliness settled in that never left him.

His dad had gone full throttle into the dating scene. Though he'd made sure Zander got a hot meal most nights, Zander got the impression his dad didn't like him much, either. They never did fun things together like his friends did with their dads. Beyond the basics, there was nothing.

By age thirteen, Zander was spending little time at home. In addition to his after-school activities, his neighborhood dog-walking business kept him plenty busy. He learned that good grades might earn him college scholarships and spending extra time with the animals got him those valuable referrals. More than either of those, he received the attention and accolades from teachers, coaches and neighbors that he never got from his father. Plus, his dad had remarried twice by that time. Wife number three came with a kid in tow. For reasons Zander never understood, his father paid attention to his ten-year-old stepsister.

After college, Zander had shared his entrepreneurial interests with his dad who, in response, discounted those ideas and urged him to work for a "solid and established" company. But Zander had wanted to build his own, so, as he'd done before, he figured it out without parental help. When Zander stopped talking about his career, the old man never asked. Their primary topic of conversation became whatever latest lady-drama plagued his father.

Zander's ringing phone snapped him back to the present, but he silenced his device and parked. Shoving aside the unpleasant memories, he headed into the building that bore his name—King Development. He entered the office suite and acknowledged his staff before powering down the hall.

When he came to a halt at the doorway to Kent Walker's office, his Senior Vice President glanced up from his laptop. "What happened?" Smiling, he shook his head. "Never mind. I can use my imagination."

"A woman's car broke down and I gave her a jump."

"*Her* or her car?"

Where Zander was driven and to the point, Kent was mellow and verbose. Friends since childhood, they'd reconnected after college. Thirteen years later, they'd turned an idea into a lucrative business, growing their two-person start-up into the region's most sought-after land development company. Despite their differences, the men remained close friends and compatible business partners.

"Give me ten to catch up," Zander said.

"I'll be gone by then. I've got to take the baby to the pediatrician for his shots. Come on in and shut the door."

This is bad. Zander closed the door and dropped into the chair across from his desk.

Kent's lighthearted expression fell away. "I hate to ask, but I need you to step in with Esteem. I can't get anyone to return my calls about their overdue payment. Can you contact the president and get us some answers?"

"Consider it done." Zander pushed up from the chair. "Is that it?"

"No. The Starry Cove project hit a major roadblock. Might be time to walk from this one."

Zander eased back down.

"I got a call from Jeremy Miller regarding the hundred-acre parcel. He and Marcia have been in support of our development proposal, but they have a personal matter and they're moving to Florida. So, they sold their fifty percent interest in the property to the other owner."

"Ah, crap. Why didn't they sell to us?"

"The terms of ownership required they give that person the first right of refusal."

"So, what...now we have to deal with that anonymous SOB who's been against the deal from the get-go?"

Pausing, Kent pursed his lips. "He's not so anonymous anymore."

"Well, that's good news, right? At least we have a name. Okay, so, we'll talk to him. Take him to dinner and—"

"The landowner is Kyle King."

Zander stilled, his gaze drilling into his business partner. No way had he heard him correctly. "I'm sorry, what did you say?"

"It's your dad, Zander."

Breaking out in a cold sweat, Zander shoved out of the chair.

"You okay?" Kent asked. "You look pasty."

"Of course I'm not okay. Are you?"

Kent held up the bottle of antacids. "I've been popping these ever since I got off the phone."

Zander shook out several tablets, tossed them into his mouth and chewed. Nausea clouded his thoughts. He had no words.

"Did you know your dad lives in Starry Cove?" Kent continued.

"Yeah. I also knew he bought the B&B when he moved there last year." Zander fisted his hands around the back of the chair.

"Did you visit him?"

"You and I go way back. You know I would've, if he had invited me."

"Right," Kent said. "Well, he's been our holdout this whole time, and now he owns *all* the land that borders the west side of town."

Zander tightened his vise grip and his knuckles turned stark white. He'd overcome professional challenges before, but this was different. This was personal. His father was all about land preservation. Kyle King despised big business. Flat-out hated it.

"According to Jeremy Miller, your dad is concerned the project will disrupt the small-town feel of the area."

"Are you kidding me? That place is a freakin' ghost town."

Kent slid his laptop into his satchel. "It's a huge loss for us. Everyone was ready to make this deal happen. Can you talk to your dad?"

Zander chuffed out a sardonic laugh. "This is playing out like a nightmare I can't wake up from. My father won't change his mind, not even for me." He massaged his forehead, hoping to silence the bass drum pounding in his head. "I'll call him, but my expectations are in the toilet."

Rising, Kent slung his computer bag over his shoulder. "I think we're going to have to stand down on this one, Zander. We have other projects where everyone's on board."

Zander tossed him a nod. "Go be a dad. We can revisit this tomorrow."

"Or never. As far as I'm concerned, the Starry Cove project is dead in the water." Kent said over his shoulder, "I'd tell you not to sweat it, but I know you will."

Zander approached his corner office and said hello to his assistant. Normally, he'd stop and chat, but he needed a moment alone. Unmotivated to check emails or return calls, he dropped into his executive chair, swiveled around and stared out the window.

Ten months ago, Zander had been approached by a group of

investors regarding a sleepy town on the Virginia-West Virginia border. The team, led by corporate magnate Colton Mitus of Mitus Conglomerate, envisioned an upscale destination getaway. Having worked with these financiers before, Zander paid Starry Cove a visit. His conclusion? A tremendous find with unlimited possibilities.

The main street was peppered with local businesses, but most had long since closed up shop and moved away. Those who'd stayed loved the area. The rural town was nestled in a valley surrounded by three mountain ranges. The Blue Ridge, the Allegheny, and the Massanutten. The geography boasted beautiful views from almost every direction. Starry Cove had the potential of becoming a vacationer's paradise.

King Development had created a master plan for the multi-use development complex designed for those who wanted to escape the hustle of the D.C. region—without having to fly anywhere. The proposal included two large hotels, an upscale boutique property with a mineral spa, a shopping outlet with over eighty stores, a twelve-theater movie complex, and a casino. Long-range plans included a deluxe condo building, but businesses would have to return to the area before they could break ground on that project.

Phase one of the multimillion-dollar complex would take eighteen months to complete, employ hundreds of workers, and bring life back to a sleepy town that had long since dropped off the map.

The investors loved his proposal, so Zander pitched it to the Starry Cove's zoning board, the local business owners, and this Miller fellow who represented the landowners. Everyone in attendance had agreed that the town needed a major infusion of business. At the time, the Millers owned fifty percent of the undeveloped land, and "anonymous" owned the other fifty.

After Zander passed the project to Kent to tie up loose ends and close the deal, the opportunity stalled. And stalled some more. The anonymous landowner had rejected the development and refused to negotiate. *And now I know why.*

The full weight of what his father had done came crashing down on him.

He wouldn't even pick up the damn phone and call me. He's known for months that we've been working to make this deal happen. How could he do this to me? Per usual, when it came to his dad, an emptiness consumed him.

Zander fished two aspirin from his desk drawer and swallowed them down. His father would never agree to anything King Development had proposed. Kent was right. The project was dead. He stared at the previous day's text from his father.

"I love you, son."

Call him. His dad's cell phone rang several times before rolling to voice mail. "Hey, Dad. Haven't heard from you in a while. Thought we could get together and talk about…" He stopped. "Give me a call." Gritting his teeth, he hung up.

Shake it off. It's not the first big deal we've lost. I need to be worried about the project I have that's costing me millions.

Zander called Anne Bickam, the president of Esteem University. When her cell phone rolled to voicemail, he called her assistant.

"Good afternoon, Office of the President," said the perky-voiced woman.

"Hello, it's Zander King for Anne."

"I'm sorry, she's in a meeting. Can I take a message?"

After Zander explained the situation, the dutiful employee suggested she transfer him to the CFO.

"That's gotten us nowhere," he replied. "I'll hold for Anne."

"Her meeting isn't scheduled to end for another forty-five minutes. If you tell me where she can reach you, I'll let her know."

Rubbing his forehead, he provided his cell phone number, then hung up. *Why can't something go smoothly today?*

It was after eleven when Zander drove home. In addition to

brooding over Starry Cove, he couldn't stop thinking about Savannah and her unreliable pickup. Did she make it to her destination or did her truck die again? Was her tan a result of her job or did she sit by the pool for hours? Her deep, sultry voice, beautiful face, and tight body appealed to him, but her determined independence was his hot button. That type of woman drove him wild.

By the time he parked in the garage of his upscale condo building, he regretted not asking for her phone number, though he doubted she would have given it to him anyway.

TWO DAYS LATER, ZANDER had sidelined the Starry Cove project, refocusing his efforts on low-hanging opportunities. But his frustration over losing *the big one* continued to gnaw at him. He left another message for his dad but, per usual, his father didn't return his call. As much as Zander disliked defeat, he filed this opportunity in the "loss" category.

While leading a conference call with a group of potential investors, his assistant set a stack of opened mail on his desk and tapped the top envelope with her fingernail.

"Important," she whispered.

When the call ended, he read the letter from a Wildflower Springs attorney.

Dear Mr. King,

It is with extreme regret that I must inform you that your father, Mr. Kyle King, has passed away. As executor of your father's estate, I'm instructed to read his will this Friday at one o'clock. If you cannot attend, I ask that you contact my office at your earliest convenience. Please accept my sincerest sympathy for your loss.

Sheldon Elstor, Esq.

As he stared at the letter, his chest tightened. The loneliness that had plagued him since childhood slammed into him like a giant tidal wave. Over the years, he'd lived with no downtime. Packing in the activities prevented him from thinking about the constant loneliness. While most mourned the loss of a parent, Zander had grieved for his a long time ago. The distant relationship with his father had been a source of great frustration. As an adult, he'd accepted it, though he never liked it.

Pushing out of his chair, he stared out the twelfth-story window, eyeing the sluggish traffic on Route 123 in Tysons. *Only sixty-four and he's gone.*

He'd last called his father on Christmas Day. Like all of their conversations, this one had revolved around Kyle's latest drama, a contentious divorce from his fifth wife, which Zander assumed had left him strapped for cash.

Concerned, Zander had sent him $25,000. A month later, he followed up because the check had never been cashed. His father had been too busy to open his mail because he'd met the love of his life.

And that's when Zander had needed a break.

Now, he would grieve what he never had—a meaningful relationship with his dad. He had no idea why his father would orchestrate a reading of his will, but he'd be there, if for no other reason than to respect his wishes and move forward, no longer expecting something Kyle King could never give him.

Returning to his desk, he lifted the receiver on his console and dialed.

"Good afternoon, the law office of Sheldon Elstor," said a soft-spoken man.

"This is Zander King. I received Mr. Elstor's letter and wanted to inquire about Kyle King's funeral services."

"Please hold, Mr. King. Mr. Elstor will be right with you."

A moment later, the on-hold music was interrupted by a different man's voice. "Hello, Mr. King. Sheldon Elstor, here. Can you make it this Friday?"

"I'll be there. I'm calling to offer financial assistance for any outstanding debts my father had."

"He's taken care of all the arrangements."

Zander paused. He thought his father was struggling financially. "Was there a funeral service?"

"No. Your father's body awaits cremation."

"How did he die?" Zander felt like an idiot for having to ask the lawyer such a basic question.

"He had a stroke."

His head hurt and he raked his fingers across his forehead. *That's rough.* "I'm sorry to hear that. Thanks for contacting me. See you Friday."

He hung up and stared at the steady stream of emails cluttering his inbox. Work was his go-to, but he was confident he couldn't stay focused today. Then, he remembered the text from his dad. *I love you, son.* Regardless of how his dad had treated him, it pained him to know that this was the end. That thread of hope he'd clung to had been permanently severed. His throat tightened and tears blurred his vision.

His assistant sailed in with a mug and set it in front of him. "I rearranged your schedule Friday."

He cleared his throat, swallowing down the grief. "That was fast. Where's Wildflower Springs?"

"About seven miles southeast of Starry Cove." Pausing, she fidgeted with her glasses. "I'm sorry for your loss."

"Thank you," he said, before sipping the hot coffee.

"I'll make arrangements for you to stay the night in Starry Cove," she continued.

He chuffed out a laugh, feeling both guilty and relieved for the momentary joy. "Where? There aren't any hotels in the area."

"The Starry Cove B&B, of course." She couldn't hide her smile, though he doubted she was trying. Subtlety was not her strong suit. "I know you and Kent consider it a dead deal, but you didn't remove the pushpin."

They eyed the large map of Virginia taped to his wall. He and Kent had marked their current projects and prospective opportunities with colored tacks. She was right. He hadn't removed the bright red pin.

"Looks like I'll be headed to Starry Cove after all."

2

SAVANNAH MORRISSETTE

THE DEATH OF SAVANNAH'S stepdad had gutted her. By the time she'd arrived at Mercy Hospital in Wildflower Springs, Virginia, his body had been moved to the funeral home for cremation. Thinking about his lifeless body sent shivers down her spine. That image was in stark comparison to the lively, quirky man he'd turned out to be.

Attempting to refocus her morbid thoughts, Savannah lifted the camera and snapped a few exterior shots of the rundown Starry Cove B&B where she was staying. When compared to the photos adorning its living room walls, the building had seen better days.

Sadly, the entire town had. The dilapidated structures lining Main Street had once been full of charm and personality, bristling with townsfolk who shopped by foot and chatted in person rather than creating relationships through texts and posts.

Click-click-click-click.

Savannah continued taking pictures, hoping the familiar activity would help soothe her. Her phone rang and she tugged it out of the back pocket of her jeans. *Ugh.* "Hi, Mom. What's up?"

Her mother had a knack for calling at the worst times. "Why do I need a reason for calling my daughter?"

Because you always do. "How's life in Vegas treating you these days?"

"What's the latest with you?" Debby King didn't answer questions. She *asked* them.

"K-Dad died."

"Who?" Her mother blew out a harsh gust of air. No doubt she was smoking.

Savannah rolled her eyes. "Kyle King."

"How did you find out? Oh, lawd, Vanna, do you think he left *me* something? Oooh, I smell money."

"You two didn't part on the best of terms."

"He always had a soft spot for you, though. Are *you* listed in his will?"

Here comes twenty questions. "Now's not a good time."

"I'll bet he included you. How much did he leave you, Vanna? *Tell me.*" A chill swept down her spine at her mother's indignant tone.

Over the years, she'd learned the best way to manage her mother was to defuse her. "Yup, you figured it out. K-Dad left me several mil. I bought a five-story estate. Stables, hot tub, a heated swimming pool *with* a hot, pool boy. Oh, and the entire thing overlooks a lake."

Her mother's biting laugh made her grimace. "Perfect timing. I'll pack up and drive cross-country next week. There's nothing going on here. Plus, I love Virginia Beach in September. You do still have that darling little house, right?"

"Uh-huh." Savannah's mind blanked. She did not want her mom to visit.

"Great! You're sad. I'm bored. We'll go shopping. Maybe pull a fast one, like old times."

Savannah's chest tightened. "Did you say *next* week?" Savannah had nothing scheduled, but a visit from her mother would *not* lift her spirits. Her phone rang with an incoming call from her agent, Tilly Mason. *Thank you, universe.* "My agent's calling. Gotta run."

"Is that woman still stealing from right under your nose? You do the work and she collects the money. Honestly, Vanna, didn't I teach you better than that?"

"Bye, Mom." Clearing her throat and the bad juju, Savannah took Tilly's call. "Hey, babe."

"Savannah, I've got good news."

"Perfect timing."

"But first, how are you doing?"

Terrible. "Hanging in. I can't believe he's gone."

"I'm sorry. I know you two were close."

"K-Dad was good to me, but his porcupine personality didn't make him a very popular guy. So, what's the good news?"

"The New Mexico Bureau of Tourism commissioned you to do a spread for their upcoming ad campaign. It's called, 'Extreme Beauty Awaits'."

Savannah's lips quirked up. "Fantastic."

Silence.

"Um…there's a tiny glitch," Tilly added.

Her smile fell away. "How bad?"

"More like, bad timing. The photographer they hired came down with Lyme disease and had to back out. The shoot is early next week, but they're willing to pay double because of their last-minute request. It's a great opportunity. Do you think you'd be up for it?"

"Hmm, let me think." She would only mope over her stepdad's passing. Now that her mom knew K-Dad was gone, Debby would definitely visit, greedy fingers outstretched. Though Savannah needed this job and the income that came with it, she wasn't confident she could manage without an assistant. "This is a big break for me. But…"

"Too soon?" Tilly asked.

"It would be easier if I had an assistant." Savannah switched the phone to her other ear and fiddled with the sterling silver ear cuff.

"Haven't found anyone yet, huh?"

"I offered the position to someone last week, but she wanted more money than I could swing."

"Hey, why don't I meet you in New Mexico and help out?"

"That would be great," Savannah replied.

"I'll book our flights. And since you'll be out there, I'll see if I can get you a meeting with Gerard Ricardo, the golf course owner who expressed interest in your work."

"The one you've been calling for months?"

"Yup."

"Keep me posted."

The call ended and Savannah headed into the B&B and upstairs to her room to change.

Over the years, Tilly had become her friend and confidant, too. The two had met at a small, private showing around the time Savannah was about to call it quits. She'd run out of money and refused to accept any more help from her stepdad. That show would have been her swan song, but the universe had other plans for her.

Tilly had loved her photographs and offered her representation. After reviewing all of Savannah's work, Tilly suggested she focus on landscapes and nature scenes. Fast-forward six years. The thirty-two year old artist had made a name for herself as a landscape photographer.

But things had changed over the past few months. Tilly had spent most of her time helping her husband run their new coffee shop. As a result, she hadn't booked a new gig for Savannah since then. In addition to hunting for an assistant, Savannah had been shopping for a new agent. Savannah hated the thought of severing their relationship, but her bank account had dwindled to fumes. Disappointment clouded her thoughts. If things didn't change, she'd have to accept the position a friend at the beach had offered her, managing a restaurant.

Savannah dressed for the meeting and left the inn. As she drove to the attorney's office, she wondered who else would be there. Material things meant little to her, so if her stepfather left her something that someone else wanted, she'd hand it over. The last thing she needed was a family feud. From what she knew, most family members didn't like Kyle anyway.

For Savannah, clothing was another form of expression, but as she glanced down at her outfit, she wondered if she'd gone overboard. *It's a reading, not a funeral.* Even so, she'd painted her canvas black. A black skirt, charcoal gray shirt, and black heels. But she'd belted her waist with a brightly flowered scarf. A tribute to the man who'd added so much color to her life.

The law office of Sheldon Elstor was located on the second floor of a quiet office building ten minutes from Starry Cove. An unremarkable brown leather sofa, matching chair, and oak coffee table with dated magazines filled the tidy waiting area.

After polite conversation, the soft-spoken receptionist led her into the conference room. "Sheldon will be right in." He left the door open and hurried back to his post.

A moment later, Sheldon walked in. "Hello, Savannah. Doing any better today?"

She rose and hugged the burly man. "I'm okay. It's been a rough couple of days…for both of us."

The sadness in his eyes mirrored how she felt. "Losing a friend is tough," Sheldon said. "Reminds me of my own mortality." He fastened on a tight smile. "Let's meet in my office."

"Am I the only one attending the reading?" she asked as they walked down the short hallway.

"No, Kyle's son Zander will be here." Sheldon gestured to one of the chairs across from his desk. "Make yourself comfortable. Excuse me a moment."

As she eased onto the hard leather seat, thoughts of Zander

warmed her cheeks. Though rarely nervous, her pulse pounded hard and fast.

She hadn't seen her stepbrother since he left for college, but man-oh-man had she crushed on him. Back then, she hid her pudgy body behind frumpy clothes and wore her oversized glasses like a shield. Being a shy ten year old, she struggled to make friends in her new school. Plus, she got tongue-tied around cute boys, especially one who was three years older and in middle school.

Once, she got up the nerve to ask him to quiz her on her spelling words, and that opened the door to more conversations. Zander liked talking about his dog-walking business and Savannah liked listening to him. She also liked looking at him. So, the more questions she asked, the more she got to stare, without getting caught.

The years passed, and Zander moved on to high school where baseball season became Savannah's favorite time of year. After school, she'd park herself at the kitchen table to do her homework and wait for him to come home. And when he did, she'd soak him up. The ends of his unkempt dark hair glistened from sweat and his lean muscles stretched against his practice uniform. She spent a lot of teenage nights tucked in bed fantasizing about her crazy-hot stepbrother down the hall.

But it was her stepfather, Kyle King, who had changed her life for the better. Their first Christmas as a blended family, he'd given her a camera. "Everyone likes looking at themselves," her stepdad told her. "Take pictures of the kids and I bet you'll make some friends."

He'd been right. Whether capturing candid moments or photographing a beautiful sunset, she found her passion. And she made a ton of friends.

After Zander left for college, she never saw him again. A year later, her mom ended the marriage, but Savannah stayed in touch with K-Dad. Most considered him a curmudgeon, but beneath that abrasive surface was a sweet man desperate to find love and always coming up short.

Savannah glanced around Sheldon's small office, the back wall of built-in shelves overstocked with law books and journals. The receptionist entered with a handsome guy in tow. Her mind stuttered to slow motion as she eyed the stranger. *It's the city slicker. Wait...that's Zander?*

"Sheldon will be right in," said the assistant. "Please have a seat." The quiet man scurried out.

Taller than she remembered and twice as muscular, Zander had traded the long, flyaway hair for a short, neat business cut. He wore a dark suit and no smile, but if memory served her, he wasn't big on smiles back then, either. Recognition flashed in his eyes, his intense gaze making her heart flutter. For a suit, he was damn fine. Damn fine, indeed.

His expression brightened. "Savannah, right?"

"Yes." Rising, she extended her hand. Savannah found the formality a necessity, but in this case, she wanted to touch him. She was as tactile as she was visual. The smoothness of his hand didn't surprise her. What did were the sparks that flew up her arm. Her type of man wore tattered jeans, a worn, old T-shirt, and sported facial hair. Tats were a bonus. She liked her men either barefoot or in dinged-up cowboy boots. Not clean cut, sporting stuffy suits and thousand-dollar shoes.

His light gray eyes stayed locked on hers. "Do you work with Sheldon?"

"No, I'm here for the reading of your dad's will."

His pleasant expression dropped, his eyes turned ice cold. "Are you one of Kyle's wives?"

"He was my stepdad."

Zander glared at her. *He thinks I'm here for a handout.*

Sheldon breezed into the room. "Mr. King, Sheldon Elstor." The two men shook hands.

Her stepbrother still hadn't cracked a smile. "Good to meet you."

"This is your stepsister, Savannah Morrissette. Well, technically she's your ex-stepsister, but we're all family here." Sheldon got comfortable behind his large, oak desk.

Zander remained steadfast. Only his jaw ticked.

"It's been a while," Savannah said to Zander. "Back then, I went by Vanna. You probably don't remember me."

The tension radiating off her stepbrother didn't surprise her. He probably had no idea she was still in Kyle's life and expected he'd be flying solo today.

"I didn't recognize you," he muttered.

"Let's get started." Sheldon opened a manila folder on his desk. They took their seats across from him.

Zander peered at her, but she kept her attention firmly rooted on Sheldon. As her stepfather's attorney began reading from Kyle's will, she glanced over. Their gazes locked, the air charged with chaotic energy. The longer he regarded her, the faster her heart banged against her chest. The uptight suit brought some heat to the meeting, something the once-shy Vanna had found very tempting.

The hunger in his eyes didn't feel adversarial. Several seconds ticked by before he turned back to Sheldon. She, however, didn't feel compelled to look away.

He parted his dark brown hair on one side and locked it down with gel. His intense gray eyes were framed by dark, jutting eyebrows. And those full lips...during her teenage years, she imagined he'd be a fantastic kisser because that fantasy—along with several others—had kept her awake night after night. Those memories heated her from the inside out. As she dragged her attention back to Sheldon, she wondered how Zander would look through the lens of her camera.

ZANDER WAS HAVING ONE hell of a time concentrating on the reading. He hadn't expected to see the sultry brunette again, and he sure as hell couldn't process his relationship to her. She didn't resemble the shy kid who'd been attached to his dad's third wife. This woman was beautiful and sexy. Seemed laid-back, too. But now that he knew who she was, he'd shove his dirty thoughts in some dark hole and bury them, *forever*.

She crossed her legs. *Nice.* She turned toward him and he slid his gaze to hers. The color had drained from her face.

"That can't be right," Savannah rasped out.

Zander snapped to attention. "Can you repeat that?"

Sheldon cleared his throat. "As sole owner and proprietor, I hereby bequeath Starry Cove Bed and Breakfast to my son, Zander King, and my stepdaughter, Savannah Morrissette, as joint tenants with rights of survivorship. I also leave them my share of the one hundred acres of unimproved land in Starry Cove under the same terms. All remaining funds are intended to be used to restore the B&B and to turn said land into a wildlife refuge that includes a nature conservancy, dog park, and walking trails that lead into town. My greatest wish is for my children to manage the project together. Zander and Savannah may elect to recommend an alternate use of the one hundred-acre parcel by mutual agreement. Please note, however, that I am against the multi-use development project proposed by King Development. I trust that my stepdaughter will honor my wishes and vote the project down."

Zander's stomach dropped while his heart shot into the triple digits. He chuffed out a grunt. "Unbelievable."

Pausing, the lawyer peered over his glasses at Zander before continuing. "My executor and close friend, Sheldon Elstor, will oversee distribution of funds for the projects. And finally, I leave my Victorian home in Starry Cove to Zander and Savannah, along with its furnishings. The home is debt free, so should they sell the estate, the funds must be divided equally."

"I wasn't expecting this," Savannah said. "It was very generous of Kyle to include me."

"He considered both of you his children, equally," Sheldon replied.

Rubbing his forehead did nothing to alleviate Zander's tsunami of a stress headache. "So, he's instructing Savannah to vote down my proposal?"

"More like 'advising', but, yes, he is," Sheldon said. "He wanted Starry Cove to retain its small-town charm."

Zander's nostrils flared. "Even after his passing, he's still trying to prevent me from completing the biggest, most lucrative project of my career."

Savannah shifted her attention from Zander to Sheldon. "Is there more?"

"Don't you think we've heard enough?" Zander quipped.

Sheldon flipped a page. "There *is* this." He began reading. "Should both heirs agree to an alternate use for the property, they have three days from the date of this reading to provide their request in writing to the executor. Neither party can sell their interest in the B&B or the land until all renovations have been completed." The attorney shifted his attention from Savannah to Zander. "That's it."

Son of a bitch. Zander was too shocked to respond. The wall clock ticked off the seconds while he digested the news that his dad had screwed him over one last time.

"If you can't return here," Sheldon interjected, "I can provide you with updates and photos of the inn during renovation, and of the nature conservancy, as well."

Zander didn't give a damn about progress reports on a dog park or a nature center.

"Keep in mind you'll have to collaborate on any and all decisions." The attorney straightened the papers. "I have an opinion if you're interested."

"No, thanks," Zander replied.

"Sure," said Savannah.

"Discuss it over a drink. You're all the family Kyle has left, and he told me he'd like for you to get to know each other."

Zander couldn't shake the utter frustration that clouded his thoughts. "With all due respect, that's not a selling point, but I agree about the drink." Zander slid his gaze to Savannah. "I'm buying."

"Sheldon, are you mediating our little family get-together?" Savannah asked.

"No. I'm confident you two can sort it out. Here are copies of the will." After handing them each a sealed manila envelope, he rose. "I'll walk you out."

Standing in reception, Zander extended a stiff arm. "I'll be in touch."

Sheldon shook his hand. "I'm sorry for your loss. If it's any consolation, your father was very proud of you, Zander."

The surprises just keep on coming.

Savannah hugged Sheldon. "I couldn't have gotten through this without your support…and Jean's, too."

"Our pleasure. I look forward to seeing those pictures."

"I'll send you the best ones. I loved the shots with your dogs. They're adorable."

Zander opened the door and, as she walked past him, she stopped and looked him dead in the eyes. "Let's go tie one on, City Slicker."

3

BLURRING THE LINES

As they left Sheldon's office, Zander's head throbbed. His father had instructed his stepsister to vote down his dream project. *Who does that?*

Had Kyle bothered to communicate his concerns, Zander would have listened. A simple conversation could have made all the difference—might have been the tipping point. His father had shunned him for the absolute last time. Now, he was determined to win if it were the last project he *ever* completed. Savannah, on the other hand, seemed unfazed. In truth, he didn't know her well enough to gauge how the news affected her.

By the time they stood on the sidewalk outside the two-story office building, Zander was fuming. Squinting, he slid on his sunglasses. "I'm staying at the Starry Cove B&B. You?"

"Ditto. I guess the inn is ours now."

"Looks that way." He forced a smile, though he was anything but happy. "There's a bar down the street from it. Let's drive back over and grab that drink." This unexpected opportunity gave him one more shot at the development, so he'd best play nice. "Can I give you a ride?"

Her gaze lingered on his for an extra beat. "I'm good. Got that new battery."

Zander spied her truck across the street. He gestured to his Range Rover. "You can follow me back, if you want."

"What happened to that flashy sports car?"

"At home."

After she eyed his vehicle, her smile snagged his attention. Easy going and sexy. *Damn, she's hot...and my stepsister. Stay on point. She needs to agree to my proposal. Period.*

"I like this one," she said. "Less pretentious."

"You're welcome to have it."

Her eyes popped wide, then she laughed.

"I wasn't joking."

"Are you trying to bribe me?"

"No. You drive a totally unreliable vehicle."

"You *are* serious. Thanks, but no."

On the ten-minute drive back to Starry Cove, he formulated a down-and-dirty game plan. Get to know her a little before proposing his development. Negotiate if necessary. Win the deal that got away. Done.

He drove onto Main Street and spotted a space in front of the restaurant. Instead of parking there, he stuck his arm out the window and pointed, then found a spot at the end of the block.

As he walked down the street, he couldn't take his eyes off her. His stepsister had filled out in all the right places. Savannah had a fantastic bust line and shapely legs. When she turned away, her sweet, tight ass hijacked his full attention. *Damn, she's hot. And completely off-limits.*

He stopped inches away. "Ready to have that drink?"

She turned around and her deep, mocha eyes locked on his. A jolt of energy surged in his chest. *Stop. She's family and I've got to work with her.*

"Definitely." Her sultry voice rumbled through him.

Determined to put distance between them, he walked to the

door and held it open. Breezing inside, she shot him a cool smile. "Thank you, brother."

The Starry Cove Bar and Grille was *the* place to be on a Friday afternoon. The saloon-style restaurant was packed. *Where'd all these people come from?* Zander spotted two empty seats at the bar. "How 'bout we grab a stool?"

"Sure thing."

A server flew by with a tray of drinks and collided with a patron. Zander snaked his arm around his stepsister and pulled her out of the way as glasses and bottles crashed onto the floor, sending liquid splashing in every direction.

Savannah's whisper-soft moan captured his attention. Rather than move away from him, she peered into his eyes. Her beauty, paired with that searing gaze, sent adrenaline streaking through him.

Conversations around the room quieted and everyone stared at the red-faced waitress. Patrons clapped while fellow servers hurried over to assist. With his arm still locked around her, Zander guided Savannah toward the bar. He *should* have removed his hand, but instead, tightened his hold around the sexy contour of her waist.

At the bar, she acknowledged him before sliding onto the seat. "Thanks."

Is she thanking me for keeping her dry, or for hauling her against me?

A burly bartender moseyed over. "How you two doin' this afternoon?"

"Doin' alright," Savannah replied. "I'll take a shot of tequila and an amber beer on draft, if you have one."

"Your best scotch, neat," Zander said, though the bartender never bothered looking in his direction.

"You two lovebirds want some food, too?"

Savannah slid her gaze to Zander and kicked up her brow. "Sure."

He bit back a smile. *Is she toying with me?*

After setting a menu on the bar between them, the bartender got busy pouring their drinks.

Savannah leaned close and peered into Zander's eyes. "Let's try not to kill each other over this, 'kay?"

The energy behind her unwavering gaze ricocheted through him. He shouldn't like staring into those hypnotic dark eyes, but he did. And he sure as hell shouldn't like this forced arrangement, but as he studied her pretty face, his throbbing headache subsided. And a different kind of throbbing took hold.

Her lips parted. She shuddered in a breath. He clenched his teeth to stem the fire burning a trail to his groin. Desiring her was wrong on too many levels. His *only* thought should be convincing her to agree to his plan for Starry Cove. But the ideas preoccupying his brain had nothing whatsoever to do with his business venture. Absolutely nothing. *Dammit, concentrate.*

The bartender dropped napkins on the bar before depositing their drinks. "Wanna start a tab?"

She dragged her gaze from Zander. "That'll work."

"What can I gitcha?"

They each ordered a burger. Savannah tacked on a side of cheese fries before the bartender moseyed off.

"So, Zander, you ready to play nice with me?" she asked.

I'll definitely play with you. Lots and lots of foreplay. He reached for his drink. "I can do that."

She lifted the shot glass. "A toast to Kyle."

He had no interest in honoring his late father, but he didn't want to start their alcohol-fueled meeting by upsetting her, so he raised his drink.

"To a sweet, funny, but misunderstood man who has been the most reliable person in my life since I was ten."

What the hell? It sounded like she was describing a totally different person from the one he knew. Before he could digest her toast, she clinked glasses and licked the salty rim. As she coated her tongue with white crystals, heat radiated through him, landing in his junk. *Get it together.*

After tossing back the liquor, she pierced him with a steely gaze. "Damn that tasted like more."

Eager to assist, the bartender appeared with the tequila bottle and a smile. Beneath his thick moustache, the dude was missing a front tooth. "I can make that happen, darlin'."

Zander didn't want him plying his stepsister with cheap booze. He needed her sober so she could agree to his proposal. Once she did, he'd draft a quick letter to Sheldon and hightail it back to civilization.

She held up her hand. "I'm good."

Relieved, he sipped his scotch. The familiar taste burned the back of his throat and he tossed back another mouthful before setting the glass down.

"Your food'll be out shortly. You just let me know if I can gitcha anything...anything at all, lil' darlin'." Before ambling down the bar, he eyed Savannah's chest.

Zander could have been on fire, and the bartender wouldn't have noticed.

As Savannah peered into Zander's eyes, her playful expression made his cock twitch. *I'm in trouble. I should have insisted Sheldon join us.*

"It's been a while," Zander said. "You look good." He hated lying. She looked sensational, but no need to go overboard.

"You too."

"Are you married? Got kids?"

"Flying solo. How 'bout you?"

"My wife's name is 'work'."

Her husky laugh rumbled through him. This sexy stepsister of his was torturing the hell out of him.

"I feel like I know you." She placed the rim of the glass to her lips and sipped the draft beer.

He dragged his gaze back to her eyes. "Why is that?"

"Your dad talked about you all the time. He hadn't heard from you in a while, but that didn't stop him from bringing you up every time we spoke."

Bullshitters infuriated Zander, but as Savannah rolled the cocktail napkin between her fingers, his gut told him she wasn't one of them.

"Then you know how important the Starry Cove development project is to my career."

"I do now, but I don't know the details." She leaned back, crossed her legs. "Lay it on me."

"My multi-use proposal will reinvigorate this town. Phase one includes three hotels, a shopping outlet, a large movie complex, and a casino. The mountain views are spectacular, the temperate climate is also a big draw. I'm looking to put Starry Cove on the map as a getaway destination. Primarily for the D.C. region, but being a stone's throw from Dulles International Airport widens the market." He tipped the glass against his lips, savoring the scotch before swallowing it down.

Her playful smile had fallen away and she tapped her fingernails on the side of the frosty glass. "I see."

"This is the biggest opportunity of my career and I don't understand why my father was so adamant about killing it without so much as a conversation." His blood pressure soared, and he loosened his tie, unfastened his top button.

As her gaze followed his movement, her lips quirked at the corners. He'd no idea what she found amusing. She tucked her short hair behind one ear revealing a small, silver cuff.

"While I can only speculate, I'm guessing he didn't want to get into it with you. I'm sure you know K-Dad is all about preserving the land. He's obsessed with it." She shook her head. "Past tense. He *was*. I keep forgetting he's gone." She bowed her head.

She's really struggling. Help her out. He wrapped his hand around her shoulder and sparks flew up his arm. "You guys were close."

After a pause, she lifted her chin. He expected tears. Instead, determination shone from her eyes. "Look, Zander, I can see this project is important to you, but I won't disrespect Kyle's wishes. The historic town should be revered, not torn down. C'mon, how many more shopping outlets does Virginia need?"

"*One* more, and this one is going to have my name written all over it," he said and removed his hand from her shoulder. Time to learn something about his stepsister that he could use as leverage. "What do you do?"

"I'm a photographer. Landscapes mostly. Shooting golf courses and state parks allows me to pay the bills."

"I'll hire you to photograph Starry Cove before, during, and after renovations are completed."

Her light-hearted laughter made him smile. "Sure, but that won't change my decision."

"We have to find common ground."

"No, we don't. I'm good with the will as it stands...although..." She paused to drink her beer. "I'm surprised Kyle didn't include renovating The Cove."

"What's that?"

"According to him, it's an abandoned drive-in movie theater that also served as a natural planetarium." She shrugged. "We can check it out after we chow down."

The bartender delivered their food. "Refills on anything, darlin'?"

"I'm good," Savannah said.

"Water for me," Zander said.

She nibbled on a cheese fry. "Mmm. Mmm, these are unreal. " Her moans weren't helping him focus on their agenda. "You've gotta try them."

She offered him one. When he took it, his fingers brushed against hers and another jolt of energy surged through him. With his gaze cemented on hers, he bit into the crispy potato. Her expression darkened, her lips parted. The tension rippling between them morphed into full-blown desire.

She shuddered in a breath. "Good, huh?"

"Yeah, very good." In truth, he had no idea how the damn fry tasted, nor did he care. All he wanted to do was run his fingers through her wavy hair and kiss her. *What the hell is wrong with me?*

The bartender placed two waters in front of them, then left without snagging Savannah's attention.

She blinked several times before refocusing on her meal. Other than exchanging comments about the burgers, they ate in silence. But he was tuned in to her every movement—she paused between bites to look around, or she'd glance in his direction and offer a casual smile. As much as her hot looks turned him on, so did her chill vibe.

Always on the go, Zander rushed from task to task without enjoying himself or the moment. While he didn't like Savannah's resistance to his project, he'd overcome obstacles before. This would be no different. What he hadn't expected was the arousing effect his stepsister would have on him. She was pushing all his buttons, especially the ones that should never be pushed by family.

Never.

When finished with her burger, she downed the last of her beer, wiped her lips with the napkin and leaned close. Her breath warmed his face and those deep, dark eyes filled him with desire.

"You have a little cheese on your lip."

She whispered the words like she was sharing a secret. Before he'd lifted his napkin, she trailed her index finger across his lower lip. As soon as she slipped her fingertip inside her mouth and sucked, the already snug space in his crotch grew tight.

Damn her. If she didn't stop, he'd have to take her somewhere, *anywhere*, and drive himself inside her until they surrendered to the ecstasy. And then, do it again because he wanted her that badly. But he couldn't bring himself to say anything beyond a long, deep moan.

She withdrew her finger. "I have a sexy confession to make."

His pulse skyrocketed. "Savannah, you're treading in dangerous waters. You know that, don't you?"

"I do." Beneath the bar, she pressed her palm against his thigh. "Say the word and I'll stop."

A tornado of passion swirled around them. Though wrong, he wanted this, wanted her. "I'm listening."

She stroked his thigh. He hardened. But more than his stiff dick, everything hinged on what she would do next. When she nuzzled his cheek, he ground out a groan. She pressed her lips against his ear.

"For years, I had the biggest crush on you. Night after night, I fantasized about you doing naughty things to me. I imagined sneaking into your room in the middle of the night and slipping into bed beside you. I wanted you to teach me how to give a blow job. I wanted your body on mine, your hardness inside me. But you didn't know I existed in *that* way."

His pulse accelerated. The need to bury himself inside her escalated to a dangerous level. Facing her, he sucked down a steadying breath. "We were family and you were a teenager."

Leaning back, she arched her brow. "Well, I'm not a teen now."

"No," he said, pinning her with a hard stare. "No, you're not."

4

THE COVE AND THE KISS

SAVANNAH WAS DONE PLAYING games. She was done doing the right thing. Despite their family connection, she wanted this man.

What harm could come from spending a few hours exploring the carnal side of her stepbrother? She might not have thought about Zander King in *that* way for a long time, but the man staring into her eyes was a much finer version of his younger self. She couldn't resist living out a fantasy that had tormented her for most of her teenage years. From the steamy look in his bedroom eyes to the sexy moan he couldn't hold back, she had every confidence he could handle her.

While she shouldn't be dragging her fingernails up and down his thick, corded thigh, she didn't want to stop. The cute, moody teenager had grown into a serious, brooding man, ten times more handsome and with the body of a Norse god.

Her world had been rocked with grief, and she wanted something more powerful than a shot of cheap tequila to dull the pain. She needed to lose herself in the arms of a man who could breathe life back into her. Zander King should *not* be that man. Any man—even the shmuck of a bartender who'd been ogling her for the past hour—would be a better choice. But she didn't want anyone else. She wanted her stepbrother.

And *only* her stepbrother.

She'd been taught that rules were meant to be broken. Was this one of them?

He paid the bill while her imagination ran wild. By the time they walked outside, her panties were damp from desire. Standing on the sidewalk, she studied his face. The tight lines around his eyes had been replaced with a searing intensity. She stepped close. He didn't back up.

After she stared into his eyes for several titillating seconds, he shook his head. "You're a beautiful woman, Savannah. But I have to put the brakes on this." His rueful smile tugged at her heart. "Sex will only complicate an already stressful situation."

Disappointment clouded her thoughts. She didn't want the day to end with her fantasy hanging out there, but he'd made his position known. "That's cool. Thanks for the grub." She widened the space between them. "I'm gonna check out The Cove."

"I don't want you going there by yourself. Do you know where it is?"

"No idea."

"Let's ask inside."

The bartender spoke directly to Savannah's breasts, but they got the directions they needed.

"I'll drive." Zander removed his jacket. Strong, hard muscles bulged against the starched white dress shirt. *For an uptight suit, he's nice. Damn nice.*

Stopping at her truck, she grabbed her shades and slung her primary camera bag over her shoulder.

After entering the location on his phone's map app, they headed north in his ultra-clean Range Rover. There was no clutter anywhere, not even a crumb. She envied that. She accumulated more crap in her vehicle and swore her car phone charger was buried somewhere in the heap. They passed an abandoned shopping center and Zander drove down a quiet country road that led to a deserted gravel parking lot. His phone rang and he silenced it.

"Go ahead and take the call."

After parking, he cut the engine. "Not now."

"This is the place," she said. "No idea where The Cove got the name, because technically it's not one." With camera bag in hand, she exited the vehicle.

The area had been marred by the disrespect of those who'd visited. Trash and empty beer bottles littered the expansive area. Graffiti covered the large, weathered movie screen. The snack shack had been bulldozed, but never cleared away. The majestic beauty of the land always inspired her, but this shit hole frustrated the hell out of her. *What a dump.*

But all was not lost. Savannah admired a pile of moss-covered boulders, overgrown trees, patches of wildflowers, and a disorderly splotch of bushes—all set against a backdrop of rolling hills.

Zander got out. "Great location for a movie complex."

I don't think so. Rather than poke the bear, she said nothing. Leaning against his Range Rover's hood, she tried picturing how the spot had once looked. And how fun it must've been to find constellations and make wishes on shooting stars.

"It's like stepping back in time," he murmured. "I never went to a drive-in. You?"

"Nope. Back in the day, they used to play movies here on the weekends. When the show ended, they'd turn off the lights. Everyone would lay on their hoods and gaze at the star-filled sky."

"How do you know this?" He rolled up his shirtsleeves and she eyed the sexy sprinkling of dark hair covering his sinewy forearms.

"Your dad told me about it when he bought the land and the B&B last year. This place has been deserted for years, but he wanted to buy it, too, and renovate it…one day."

Standing beside her, Zander leaned against the front of his SUV and regarded the area. "Tell me about your relationship with him."

She paused. *Where to begin?* "He was quiet, like you. I liked that about him because my mom talked *nonstop.* When she and I moved in with you guys, I struggled to make friends. That first Christmas, he bought me a camera, suggested I take pictures of the kids. His advice changed my life."

The late afternoon sun cast long shadows, and her trigger finger itched to capture how the light bounced off the hills in the distance. She pulled out her camera, set the bag on the ground, and perched her sunglasses on top of her head. Then, she snapped a few shots. For Savannah, shooting pictures was like opium to an addict.

"I see." His biting tone snatched her attention. His lips were slashed in a thin line, his eyes narrowed.

Should I stop? While mulling what to say, she leaned against the hood and studied the landscape.

He rested his hand between her shoulder blades. "My issues with my father are my own. Please continue."

While she assumed his touch was intended as brotherly, electrifying waves of pleasure scurried through her. She ached to run her fingers through his hair and feel the silky strands tickle her skin, then crush her mouth on his. Instead, she played with the shutter speed. "He helped me pay for college and encouraged me to continue with photography when I wanted to quit."

"It's good to know he could be supportive." Again his phone rang and he silenced it.

"Maybe K-Dad didn't show it, but he loved you."

Zander slipped his hand—the one that had been touching her —into his pants pocket and stared at the ground.

A fluffy white cloud kept the sunlight from reflecting off his face. She adjusted the aperture and raised the camera. Studying him through the viewfinder gave her a different perspective.

Beyond the obvious chiseled features and strong lines of his contoured face, she saw something she hadn't been able to see with her own eyes.

His sadness.

And her heart broke for the man who'd wanted something he would never receive. She'd unintentionally glimpsed his most private, innermost feelings, and she lowered the camera.

A few seconds passed before he faced her. And that's when everything changed. His gaze laid her bare. His jagged breathing roared in her ears. When his long fingers caressed the back of her neck, she shivered from the excitement of his skin on hers. His touch was strong, yet gentle, the mixture of the two lighting her insides on fire.

Though the clouds stole the warmth of the day, his radiating heat seared her. The space between them turned electric, like the charged atmosphere before a lightning strike.

"I want you, Zander."

"Savannah." His cutting tone turned her nipples hard.

Despite her pounding heart, her breathing shallowed. When she placed her hand on his hard thigh, her fingertips tingled.

His breath caught, his eyes never leaving hers. *Kiss me, Zander.*

"Hell, you are too damn sexy." He pushed off the hood and trapped her in his arms.

She gasped. When his mouth found hers, the intensity was euphoric. His raw, sensual kiss was anything but brotherly. This was the kiss of a man who wanted more, needed more, and could give her so much more.

Their embrace turned greedy. She raked her fingers through his hair and down his back. As soon as she ground against him, he nipped her lip. His hardness pressed against her and she moaned. *My God, he feels good.*

When she grasped his hand and placed it over her breast, he groaned. His thumb grazed her hardened nipple through her shirt and he massaged her womanly flesh.

"Mmm," she murmured.

Suddenly, he ended their embrace and stepped back, the abrupt separation leaving her cold. "Hell, I want you so damned badly. But we're family and this is wrong."

Dizzy from the rush of endorphins, she caressed her swollen lip. Her thoughts blurred as she fought the urge to go to him. Gasping for air, she struggled to get it together.

A few seconds passed before she could speak. "You and I couldn't be more different. You're all about land development. I'm about preserving the environment. You want to build a glitzy stop-n-shop and I want to honor Kyle's wishes. You're an uptight suit and I'm a carefree spirit. But we *are* in agreement on one thing. Hooking up would be wrong. Very, very wrong."

Verbalizing the truth only made him that much more desirable. Every now and again she liked being a bad girl. But this? This was beyond bad. This crossed into reckless. Savannah didn't mix sex with business. *Ever.* If there was anything she valued, it was earning her chops in the male-dominated world of landscape photographers. Even though Zander wasn't a part of that world, K-Dad had entrusted her to carry out his wishes in a weighty business deal. Sex would further complicate their adversarial situation.

Despite her logical reasoning, a smile tugged at the corners of her mouth. Her beautiful stepbrother was mighty, mighty fine and oh-so-tempting. *Better to back off.*

Kneeling, she tucked her camera back into the bag. When she rose, his lids were heavy, his eyes dark with desire.

"We crossed a line." He cleared his throat. "I don't do impulsive."

"Never?"

"No, never."

My God, he's uptight. "Hmm, might be good for you."

He glared at her.

"Relax, Slick. It was one kiss and a fleeting thrill for my tit. It won't happen again. Why don't we make things simple and not touch each other again?"

"Agreed."

"Should we seal it with another kiss?" She laughed alone.

He hitched a brow. "We've got legal and business issues to iron out. If that's not enough, we—no, check that—*you* need to return to The Town that Time Forgot and sort through Kyle's things."

She chuckled. Uptight suit had a delightfully dry wit after all. "It's a charming, old Victorian home. Don't you like it?"

"I've never seen it."

"Well, we'll have to remedy that."

"You can have anything and everything in that house. I have no intention of going there."

As Savannah slid into the Range Rover, she started to protest, but a sly smile graced her lips. Zander King lived in a world of absolutes. He didn't do impulsive, *ever*. She could have *everything* in Kyle's home because he was *never* going there. While his conviction was admirable, she wondered what his life would look like if he weren't wound so damn tightly all the time.

5

GOTTA RUN

As SAVANNAH AND ZANDER entered the Starry Cove B&B, she inhaled the musty scent and eyed the quaint furnishings. *Hard to believe this is mine. Well, half mine.*

Before checking in, Zander slowed to a stop. "We'll have to evaluate the structure of the building. Make joint decisions regarding what and when to renovate." His phone pinged with an incoming text.

She peered up at him. "You're a busy guy."

Tight lines around his eyes deepened. "Lots of fires to put out lately. After I deal with work, let's discuss next steps." He glanced around. "Down here."

She wanted to climb him, not talk to him. "Sure."

Again, Zander's phone rang. "What the hell?" Like earlier, he silenced it.

"Why don't you see why your phone is blowing up? Let's meet in, say, an hour."

"Savannah." His deep timbre, paired with the intensity behind his gaze, held her full attention. What was it about this man that made him so irresistible? "I hope we can work through our differences."

Truth was, she was just another business transaction on his radar. "See ya." She stopped at the base of the stairs and turned back. He hadn't moved. Across the room, his smoldering stare drilled into her. Beyond his obvious good looks, their connection tugged at her heartstrings. Or was she imagining something that wasn't even there?

As she walked to her room, her chest tightened. She'd crossed a line with a searing kiss and would have crossed several more if Zander hadn't been the voice of reason. *I need an objective opinion.*

After entering her room, the silence magnified how alone she was. She set her camera bag on the bed, dug her phone from her handbag, and tapped the home button, but the phone stayed dark. "Ugh, come on, Savannah."

Per usual, she'd forgotten to charge it. Rummaging through her belongings, she yanked out the charger and plugged it in.

While it juiced up, she glanced around the cozy room and did a double take. *How'd I miss those?* The two, framed photographs that hung on the back wall were hers. One was a Virginia Beach sunrise and the second was a Shenandoah Mountain sunset. *Did K-Dad hang my work in all the rooms?* Her stepdad had supported her in ways she never knew. *What a dear, sweet man.*

Her phone lit up and binged with unanswered calls. Ignoring them, she dialed. "C'mon, babe. Pick up."

"Savannah, finally," said her agent, Tilly. "I've got great news."

"I kissed my stepbrother."

"Like a peck?"

"No. The mind-blowing, take-no-prisoners kind. And I wanted to take things further."

"You don't mean sex, do you?"

"Um…yeah."

"Ooookayyyyy. So, um, *wow.* Can we blame alcohol?"

"Nope."

"Is this a condition of the will or something?"

Savannah laughed. "God, no. He's this uptight suit. Not my

type at all. Even so, I'm crazy attracted to him. Always have been. The man is gorgeous, but it's more than that. I like his anal personality, too. Plus, he's driven to the point of making himself insane. Strangely, I'm drawn to that, too. And, my God, he's built like an oak and all I wanna do is climb him. Whew, he's hot. Tilly, I've lost it. I'm babbling. I don't babble."

Tilly laughed. "No, you don't. You must have it bad for this guy. And you're telling me because?"

"You know I don't mix biz with pleasure. Talk me off the ledge."

"But he's not a photographer."

"K-Dad left us property and land we have to manage *together*."

"I've known you for years and you've *never* reacted like this. You're not related. Why not have a little fun?"

"Not helping."

"Sorry, honey. Look, you're going through a tough time. Don't beat yourself up because you aren't thinking clearly. Just move on."

"No can do. Zander doesn't like the arrangements, so I've agreed to meet with him. And stare at him…one of my favorite pastimes."

Tilly chuckled. "Well, that meeting with your beautiful stepbrother will have to wait. Let's circle back to the *zillion* calls I left you. I got you another job, well, a *possible* job, but you're a shoo-in. Anyway, you're flying out tonight."

Savannah's stomach dropped. "*What?*" Though normally excited for new gigs, she didn't want to leave. Not yet.

"I actually spoke with Gerard Ricardo. When I told him you'd be in Albuquerque, he *finally* agreed to speak with you about photographing his golf courses. This is such a great opportunity for you."

"I'll meet with him as soon as I'm finished with the tourism shoot."

"He's heading out of town Sunday and, because I pleaded, he's squeezing you into his schedule tomorrow morning. I booked you on a flight out of Dulles tonight. You gotta hit the road, now."

Savannah didn't want to bolt before seeing Zander one final time. But shooting Gerard Ricardo's world-renowned courses could be *the* career changer.

"I'll be outa here in ten." With a heavy heart, she hung up. Then, she called the front desk and asked for Zander's room. When he didn't answer, she collected her bags and hurried down to the front desk.

"Checking out ahead of schedule?" asked the clerk.

"Unfortunately, yes." Savannah dug a business card from her camera bag and scribbled a note. "Could you please see that Zander King gets this?"

"Absolutely." The clerk took the card. "Safe travels."

"I like Starry Cove. Maybe I'll get back here one day."

HOPING TO QUELL HIS thundering headache, Zander stood beneath the hot shower unable to shake Savannah from his thoughts. Her sultry lips had molded to his while she'd dug her nails into his shoulder blades and ground against him. It had taken all his efforts to refuse her. As the water pounded his back, he wondered if he'd made the wrong decision.

Don't go there. She's your stepsister.

From what he knew of her, they were polar opposites. He was driven. She was chill. He'd rooted himself in Northern Virginia. She roamed the countryside like a gypsy. He was analytical, she a creative type. Despite his passion for winning, he envied her laid-back attitude.

Ignoring his hard-on, he turned off the faucet and toweled dry. Zander had three days to make his case and one person's mind to change. The sooner he could sell Savannah on developing Starry Cove, the quicker he could move the project to the win column.

Since she'd been interested in The Cove, he'd tag that on as an actionable item. Restoring the drive-in might earn him some points with his nature-loving stepsister.

The project that got away. Only it didn't...yet.

With a game plan in place—and a commitment to keep his hands off her—he dressed before sitting on the edge of the bed to read the string of texts. Two women he'd taken out had expressed interest in getting together over the weekend. He skipped those and replied to the more urgent, work-related texts.

Leaning back against the propped pillows, he played back his voice messages.

Message one from Kent. "Word got out that we might declare bankruptcy. I tried reassuring everyone, but we've got some folks freaking out. Big time." Kent's tight voice and fast speech a sure sign he was beyond frustrated.

No reason to panic.

The next three messages were from anxious King Development executives and he replied to each with a text, hoping to calm things down. "Bankruptcy doesn't mean we're definitely going out of business. Restructuring our financial situation will put us back on a path to a positive cash flow." *No effing way will I file for bankruptcy. We've been in tight spots before and I'll get us out of this one, too.*

Message five was from his assistant. "Zander, I emailed you a Wall Street Journal article about Esteem University being investigated by the SEC."

After tapping the link, he read the story. Other than some conjecture about financial statements, few details were given. He scraped his fingers down his whiskered cheek. *That can't be good.*

He forwarded messages six, seven, and eight to his assistant and left word for her to handle.

Message nine was from Kent's wife, Megan. "Kent's in the hospital. Call me as soon as you get this."

Jesus, no. Zander's guts twisted. He called her back, but got voicemail, so he sent her a text. "Got your message. Call me ASAP."

He tried Kent directly. The phone rang almost a dozen times before Kent's voicemail picked up. Zander hung up and sent a text. "Are you OK? What happened?"

He listened to the remaining messages. Two more women were looking for a Friday night companion. But rule-following Zander King didn't want anyone else. He wanted his sultry, soulful, sexy, independent stepsister who spoke her mind, didn't hold back, operated on impulse, and rocked his ever-predictable world. The only living person he could call 'family'. *What a cluster.*

He texted Megan again. "I'm concerned about Kent." While waiting for her to get back to him, he leaned against the propped pillows.

ZANDER JERKED AWAKE. TEMPORARILY confused, he glanced around the room, then checked the time on his phone. Almost three in the morning. "Dammit." *Savannah must think I blew her off.*

Nothing could be further from the truth. He wanted to wake her and apologize, but he wouldn't stop at an apology. Not at three in the morning. He'd stop when he'd finished ravaging her. *I'll explain at breakfast.*

After undressing, he slid beneath the cool, crisp linens. Before switching off the light, he surveyed the room. Faux candles illuminated the fireplace mantle, a basket of apples and oranges were neatly arranged on the small table, and a welcome note lay unread. Two framed photographs hung on the wall. One, a field of bright, red poppies, and the second, a beach sunrise.

The rustic, old-fashioned charm appealed to him.

As he drifted back to sleep, his thoughts returned to Savannah, the beautiful strong-willed temptress who stood between him and the biggest development project of his career, not to mention the solvency of his company.

Despite knowing the difference between right and wrong, Zander wasn't sure how to handle what had happened. Kissing her fell squarely in the "wrong" category. And he couldn't deny that wanting her was plain insane. He resolved that crossing that line could *never* happen again.

His phone alarm woke him. Six o'clock. He pushed out of bed and padded into the bathroom. After getting ready, he called Kent.

"Good morning," Kent said. "How's Starry Cove?"

"Work can wait. What happened to you?"

"Slight setback, but I'll be fine."

"What does that mean?"

"It means I had a heart attack. There was a small blockage. I've got a stent now, so I'm good as new."

Zander's stomach dropped. "Jesus, are you okay?"

"Yes, provided I make the obvious life changes. Exercise, better eating. Doc said stress is a real killer, so Megan has ordered me to cut back on work."

"Good call. Is she with you?"

"Yeah, she's been amazing. Her folks have been watching the kids and she hasn't left my side. I just sent her down to the café for breakfast. She's scared, but she's trying to hide it. On the flip side, she did threaten to kill me if I don't learn how to pace myself and slow down. Her new favorite word is 'chill'."

"Listen to your wife. Rest up and I'll stop by the hospital when I get back."

"I'm being discharged later today or first thing tomorrow. Come by the house."

"I'm sorry this happened, Kent. What can I do to help?"

"This is a wake-up call for *both* of us, my friend. You're wound as tightly as I am...maybe worse. Time to make some serious adjustments."

No effin' way. "Take care of yourself. Give Megan my best." Zander ended the call and grabbed his laptop.

Time to tackle the issues of the day, starting with Savannah.

He drafted an email to his father's attorney detailing the Starry Cove multi-use complex. He included a brief paragraph reiterating how the expansion would stimulate existing business owners and lure previous ones back. To sweeten the deal, he added a complete restoration of the drive-in movie theater at The Cove.

With the investors lined up, he was eager to break ground. All he needed was a willing partner. And he'd have that once his stepsister co-signed his email. Determined to change her mind over breakfast, he left his room.

En route to the dining room, he passed the front desk. The clerk greeted him with a cheery smile. "Good morning. Sleep okay?"

"Very comfortable bed."

"Your friend left this for you." She held out a business card. "She rushed out last night."

SHE'S GONE? He took the card.

Zander—
Sorry I had to run. Got a gig in Albuquerque.
Call me to work out the Starry Cove details.

He whipped out his phone and called her, but got voicemail, so he hung up and sent her a text. "It's Zander. Call me ASAP."

If she hadn't charged her phone, she might not get his text before the three-day deadline on Monday. His guts churned. Beyond his unwillingness to walk from the Starry Cove project, never seeing Savannah again left him feeling unsettled.

Panicking wasn't his style, so he continued into the dining room and ate breakfast.

When he finished, the server cleared his plate. "Someone liked the French toast."

"It was delicious."

"Fruit and vegetables we serve here come from local farmers," said the gray-haired woman. "Everyone around here is like family."

She chatted about the town, steeped in history and allegiance. His server was the fourth generation of Smiths to live in the area.

"Does anyone miss the drive-in movie theater?" he asked.

"We all sure did love that place. That was something we did every Saturday night, except when the snow stopped us from getting out." She leaned closer. "Rumor has it that a big-name developer from D.C. wants to turn our town into some sort of high-roller resort. I'm not wild about a casino, but if we want to stay afloat, we could use a facelift."

"I'll take that into consideration."

Her cheeks turned tomato red. "Oh, my gosh. Oh, my goodness."

Zander offered a reassuring smile. "I'm Zander King, Kyle's son."

She swallowed. "Hello, Mr. King. Have a just talked myself out of a job?"

"It's Zander and, no, not at all. I appreciate your honesty."

"I'm sorry for your loss. Let me know if you have any questions about the inn." She took his plate, wished him a safe journey, and scooted toward the kitchen.

Before checking out, Zander examined the structure. The run-down B&B needed more than a cosmetic touch-up. In addition to the chipped paint, peeling wallpaper, and warped floorboards, heat from the kitchen spilled into the dining room, but the air conditioner couldn't keep up.

On the way upstairs to collect his bag, he examined the building from a structural perspective. Despite needing some shoring up, there was no denying the old-style, Victorian charm. *Maybe Savannah's right about preserving Starry Cove's historic essence.*

Driving home, Zander pulled up the mobile number for the president of Esteem University.

"Hello," said Anne Bickam.

"Anne, it's Zander King, King Development. You've been hard to track down."

"Zander, good to hear from you. How are you?"

"I'm calling about the first payment against our loan."

Silence.

"It's thirty days past due," Zander continued.

"I'm surprised that hasn't been paid. We've got a lot going on right now, I'll check into that first thing Monday."

Zander despised getting the runaround. "Look, Anne, my senior VP has made multiple calls to your CFO with no response. I'm going to assume that since Esteem hasn't paid the first loan payment, the second one—due this week—won't be paid, either."

"I'm sure there's just a little mix-up." If her nervous laughter was meant to downplay the problem, it had backfired.

"Unfortunately, I'll be alerting my team to stop work on the project effective immediately. If we don't receive both installments by Wednesday, we'll take legal action to recover the funds. You don't want *that*, do you?"

"Zander, really. I think you're overreacting."

"Call it whatever you want, Anne. Deadline is Wednesday." He ended the call.

In his ensuing series of calls, Zander spoke with his VP of Operations, left a message for his Chief Financial Officer, and touched base with his in-house attorney. Zander didn't like being the bad guy, but a hundred and twenty-five million dollar loan was a significant chunk of change. If he didn't play hardball, they'd continue to take advantage of the situation. *Not happening.*

Next, he spoke with two of his execs about the bankruptcy rumors. Nervous employees wanted guarantees. Despite his efforts to allay their fears, he couldn't make any promises. Morale and productivity were in the toilet. Everyone was too busy talking about the *possibility* of bankruptcy to get any work done. Frustration burned a trail to his gut.

Then, he called his HR Director.

"I'm going to be frank with you," she said. "You're going to lose employees, possibly in key positions. Goes with the territory. That'll improve our cash flow, but we'll have to backfill, which brings us full circle."

"Attrition might buy us time."

They spoke for a few more minutes before Zander ended the call.

Driving east on Route 7, he glimpsed the sign for the Dulles Toll Road. *Do it.* Spontaneity wasn't his forté, but he veered onto the ramp toward the airport. He had no game plan, no back-up strategy, and no idea where in the hell he'd find Savannah when he landed in New Mexico. But he didn't care. He needed to see her.

Twenty minutes later, he strode into the busy terminal. Despite demanding routine and order, his world was in a shambles. He'd lost the Starry Cove project because his father wanted to preserve nature more than he wanted his son to succeed. His company teetered on bankruptcy, and his longtime business partner was dealing with a serious health issue, leaving Zander to pick up the slack. *Let's not forget about kissing my stepsister.* His jaw ticked. He couldn't handle any more stress. *Step one: Find Savannah.*

While waiting in line for a ticketing agent, he called his stepsister. Before the call connected, an available agent's hand shot up. "Next," she called out.

Zander hung up and approached the counter. "Good morning. I need a one-way ticket to Albuquerque."

And just like that, he thrust himself headfirst into the fray.

6

THE ASSISTANT

Z ANDER OPERATED BEST WHEN he had explicit plans. Unfortunately, when the plane touched down at half past twelve in Albuquerque, he had none. His phone blew up with messages and texts, but there was nothing from Savannah.

Inside the terminal, he sifted through his bag for the manila folder from Sheldon and called the number on the attorney's letterhead. From what he'd surmised, Sheldon had a personal relationship with Savannah. Maybe he knew his stepsister's whereabouts. An outgoing message indicated the law office would open at eight thirty the following business day. No cell phone number was provided. He scrutinized Sheldon's website for one, but none was listed. *Dammit.*

He wouldn't run half-cocked into the city, so, until he could formulate next steps, he'd stay put. After grabbing coffee, he found a row of chairs facing the tarmac and eased onto the faux leather seat. Planes thundered by, but his phone stayed quiet. He had no idea what job Savannah booked or who else to contact for her whereabouts. Gazing out at the impressive mountain range, he acknowledged his bone-headed move. *This is why I don't do impulsive.*

Frustrated, he texted Savannah again. When no dots appeared, he dialed her number. *This time I'll leave her a damn message.*

A woman crossed in front of him, pointed to the empty chair beside him, and dropped her bags on the floor. "Sit. Both of you."

Two young boys pushed and shoved into the seat, jockeying for more room.

The mom knelt, her cheeks flushed. "One of you can sit near the window on the trip to your cousins' and the other on the flight home. If you can't stop arguing with each other, we're not going. Is that what you guys want?"

"I wanna go," whined the younger one.

Savannah's outgoing message hijacked Zander's attention. "If you can't reach me, call my agent, Tilly Mason." Savannah rattled off a phone number as one of the boys squealed.

"Ow, that hurt! Mom, he pinched me."

"Sorry," the mom said to Zander.

"It's okay." Ending the call, Zander smiled at the boys. "Hey, guys. Where you headed?"

"To visit our cousins," said the older one.

"You two are lucky to have each other," Zander said. "I'm an only child. I don't have a buddy to hang with."

"Nobody to play with?" asked the younger one.

Zander shook his head. "I'm all alone."

"That's sad," said the older brother.

"It doesn't matter who sits near the window," Zander said. "What's important is that you get to sit next to each other."

"Okay." The older one took the younger one's hand. "You can sit near the window if you want."

Rising, the mom mouthed, "Thank you," before addressing her sons. "Everybody calm?"

Nodding, the kids scrambled off the chair, and the trio left.

Zander called Savannah again. As soon as he heard the agent's number, he hung up and dialed. *Come on, answer.*

"Hello?"

Yes! "Is this Tilly Mason?"

"Depends on who's calling."

"This is Zander King, Savannah's stepbrother."

"Oh, hey. And yes, this is Tilly. Savannah mentioned that she… um…that you guys…um…er, I'm surprised to hear from you."

"I flew to Albuquerque to talk with her, but can't reach her. Do you know where she is?"

"She left me a message from her hotel. She lost her phone. Wait, did you say you're there, now?"

"Yes." He gritted his teeth. "Where can I find her, Tilly? I'm short on time and it's important."

"Hmm," Tilly replied. "I ran into a little snag myself. Maybe we can help each other out."

―――――――

SITTING AT A PATIO table overlooking the pristine golf course, Savannah sipped a sparkling water while Gerard flipped through her portfolio. The first half of their meeting had gone well. He'd escorted her through the members-only clubhouse showing her the outdated collection of framed photos that covered the walls. She'd asked open-ended questions to understand his vision. Gerard wanted what most club owners wanted—breathtaking pictures that captured the natural beauty of his PGA-ranked golf courses. She pointed out a few shots in her portfolio that she'd replicate for his properties.

"These are exactly what I had in mind," Gerard said. "What are your fees?"

For a brief second, she hesitated. *Why didn't Tilly discuss my rates with him?* After explaining her pricing structure and the estimated number of days she'd need to complete the job, she shut up. Another tactic she'd learned from her agent.

His smile dropped. "That's much more than I'd expected to pay. I'd like to hire you, but I can only offer half your rate."

Her chest tightened. In the past, Savannah caved when her clients challenged her daily rates. She wouldn't push back, never stood her ground. Once Tilly joined her team, she learned she was being taken advantage of. Tilly doubled her fees and wouldn't back down. *C'mon, woman up.*

Swallowing down her insecurity, she forced herself to continue.

"Gerard, what do you tell someone who's interested in a membership, but thinks your fees are too high?"

The club owner chuckled. "I suggest he or she golf elsewhere and compare."

"Great advice. My rates are based on my expertise and my time. Which one should I forgo in order to charge you half my fee?" Though she didn't break eye contact, her mouth had gone dry.

As Gerard glanced down at her open portfolio, Savannah fiddled with her earring cuff. *Deep breath.*

"Well said," he replied. "I'll give your proposal serious consideration. Unfortunately, I have to rush off to another meeting. I'll be out of town next week and will touch base when I get back." He extended his hand. "Thanks for coming by."

Dammit. I should have countered. Forcing a smile, she shook it. "This course is beautiful. I'd love to photograph all three."

Gerard pulled a business card from his pocket. "Please stay. Lunch is on the house." He spoke to a wait staff before retreating into the building.

Not winning this job had sealed her fate. After the tourism gig, she'd return home and accept the restaurant job at the beach. For now, Savannah would drown her sorrows in something stronger than the sparkling water she'd been nursing.

"Great job standing your ground." The deep, sexy voice behind her sent jolts of energy scurrying through her.

She spun around and her heart leapt into her throat. *Ohmygod, it's him.* Zander sat at the table behind her, oozing his private brand of confident sophistication and brimming with raw sensuality. Despite her wildly beating heart, she wasn't going to let on he'd just rocked her world. He hadn't hunted her down in New Mexico to pay her a social call, and she had no intention of caving to his demands simply because he'd flown halfway across the country to see her.

Her lips curved. "Small world, Slick."

"Hello, Savannah." His husky voice, coupled with that devilish gleam, made her tremble.

She gave him the once over. Dark tailored suit paired with a light pink dress shirt. No tie. She wanted to run her tongue over the exposed skin on his chest and taste every delicious inch of him. *Does he know he brings the heat every damn time? He's gotta know.* "I didn't peg you for an eavesdropper." She kicked out the chair Gerard had vacated.

With drink in hand, he rose. His movement was deliberate, calculated. He held her in his sights like a raptor tracking its prey. Tilting her head, she soaked up all his masculine hotness. Those deliciously broad shoulders giving way to a wide chest and a nice, tight torso. Bulging thighs pressed against the dark dress pants.

Pinning her with an unwavering gaze, he leaned down. Her insides tightened in anticipation of his kiss, his warm, minty breath heating her down to her toes. But he stopped shy of her cheek.

"My bad," he murmured. "I almost kissed you hello. We can't have that, now, can we?"

Had her uptight stepbrother changed his tactic? Traded his aggressive approach for a more playful one?

Though her heart hadn't stopped banging against her ribcage, she offered nothing more than a sly smile. "No, we can't." She pointed to the empty chair. "Sit."

After easing down next to her, he raised his glass. "Congratulations. You didn't back down when Gerard challenged your fee."

"I didn't counter, either."

"He doesn't negotiate his rates. Why should you?"

Zander had a point. Pausing, she studied his face. Beyond the gorgeous angles, chiseled cheekbones, and those beautiful translucent eyes, worry lines forged deep craters between his brows. But the dark stubble running along his jawline gave him a sinfully sexy look.

"So," she said, playing things cool. "What brings you to the land of enchantment?"

His gaze darkened. "You."

As they stared into each other's eyes, blood whooshed through her veins. She shouldn't be so damned glad to see him. In fact, she should be outright pissed that he'd shown up while she was working. *Who does he think he is, anyway?*

The waiter provided Zander with a place setting, set down two lemon-infused waters, and dropped off menus.

"I owe you an apology," he said when the server left.

"For what?"

"I fell asleep last night."

She let out a low chuckle. "You did *not* fly across the country to tell me *that*."

"No, I didn't."

Leaning back, she crossed her legs. "Look, *brother*, I am dead-set against commercializing that darling, little town by adding a casino and a zillion outlet stores. So, unless you have something *else* in mind, you can take your fancy duds and glitzy shoes, and hop the next flight back east."

"Not happening." He raked his long fingers down his scruff. "Turns out, that's not the only reason I'm here."

"Oh, this oughta be good."

"I'm assisting you this weekend."

What? Though a ripple of need skittered through her, Savannah barked out a laugh as the server set tortilla chips and a trio of salsas on the table. He pointed to each bowl. "The heat level goes from mild to spicy hot."

She eyed Zander. *It sure does.* "I'll take a double shot of tequila," she said to the server.

"We have to work," Zander said. "How about an iced tea or an Arnold Palmer?"

"We have both," said the server.

Savannah grunted her exasperation. "I'll have an Arnold Palmer."

"Another iced tea," said Zander.

When the waiter left, she slid her gaze to his. "I was mistaken about you."

"Why's that?"

"You do have a sense of humor."

"No, actually, I don't."

He's serious? She stared at him, still in disbelief. "Assist me with what?"

"Tilly can't get here until next week. Her husband has a coffee shop emergency. Something about water everywhere. Since she can't help you prep for the shoot, she asked me to step in."

"I'm not following. Why do I need help with prep?"

"The artistic director couldn't reach you, so she contacted Tilly. They want you to check out potential locations *before* shooting begins Tuesday. They've emailed you a list."

Goose bumps erupted on her arms. "Are they pushing back the start date?"

"Not according to Tilly, which is why she asked me to assist. I haven't seen the email, but she mentioned there are a dozen places they want you to visit."

Her palms grew moist. "So, I'm stuck with you?"

"Afraid so." He looked pretty damned smug.

She eyed his clothing. "Well, you aren't working for me dressed like *that.*"

He glanced at his suit. "I'll wear whatever you want under one condition."

"*You're* putting conditions on *me*?"

"We stop at a wireless store and buy you a phone."

Refusing to give him the satisfaction of admitting she'd lost hers, she bit back the smile and waited. Surely he'd toss out another condition or ultimatum regarding Starry Cove. He did not. She studied him while weighing her options. His poker face served him well. He gave nothing away. Maybe she could learn a thing or two about business from the king of all things. If she sent him home, she'd be forced to scout locations alone and stew over losing Gerard's business. But if she agreed to his help and put him to work, what would she owe him at the end? A casino? A shopping outlet?

Keeping him around was a gamble. But she'd been backed into a corner and needed his help. Shifting in the chair, she hitched a brow. "I can be a demanding woman, especially when it comes to my work."

"I'll rise to the challenge." He flashed a grin. "You'll see. I'm a very hard worker."

She extended her hand. "Deal."

They stared into each other's eyes as they shook on it, and she warmed to his touch. Was he tempting her or teasing her? In either case, she was up for the challenge. *Game on, brother.*

The server barged in to deliver their beverages. After taking their sandwich orders, he asked if there was anything else they needed.

"Yeah," she replied. "Is there a place we can pick up some western-wear for my dapper, new assistant?"

7

LOOK BUT DON'T TOUCH

A N HOUR LATER, ZANDER stood on the sidewalk dressed in blue jeans, a wrinkled white shirt—because the salesman had assured him that "crinkled" was in—and cowboy boots. He hadn't worn denim in over a decade, nor had he *ever* considered owning genuine cowhide boots. But he was a man of his word. If his stepsister wanted him to look like a ranch hand, then, by God, he would.

From what he could tell, she liked bossing him around. Surprisingly, he liked it, too. In the end, he bought a couple of pairs of jeans and a few shirts. In exchange for his cooperation, she heaped her undivided attention on him. That alone was worth every penny spent. When it came to his striking, all-business stepsister, he was hooked.

After tossing the shopping bags in the Jeep, he spied a coffee shop. "As much *fun* as that shopping excursion was, it's time to get to work. Are we ready now?"

Stepping back, she hitched her hands on her curvaceous hips, and nodded. "Now, you look like a photographer's assistant. And yes, I am ready."

So am I, in every way imaginable.

"How about we grab some joe and review your client's email?" he suggested.

While standing in line, she fiddled with her new phone, one that could hold a charge for days. Though she'd resisted, he bought her several accessories. Going forward, she might not remember to use them, but she had them at her disposal.

Zander's thoughts returned to his earlier conversation with Tilly. She'd explained that Savannah hadn't had an assistant in over eight months and scouting new places alone stressed her out, especially when challenged with a tight timeframe and a new client.

In light of those issues, he'd shelve any conversation about Starry Cove until Savannah was better prepared for her shoot. He respected that, in spite of the obvious hurdles, she'd accepted the booking.

Timing couldn't have been worse. With Kent in the hospital, Zander had asked his Operations VP to be on point for any weekend emergencies. Then, he told his shocked assistant he'd be out of pocket until Monday. Megan promised to call if there were any changes in Kent's health.

Though Zander had silenced his phone's ringer, his thigh vibrated with every new email and text. Never before had Zander relinquished control of King Development, and he fought the continual urge to see what was going on.

If that wasn't enough of a challenge, he was having one hell of a time abiding by their no-touch rule. Despite how fantastic Savannah looked in her ass-hugging jeans and that bright-pink tank top, he wasn't going to lay a finger on her. God help him. He was not.

With iced coffee drinks in hand, they found a cozy table tucked in the corner.

As Savannah read him her client's email, her shoulders tensed at the long list of possible locations she'd been asked to visit. They'd provided seven in Albuquerque and tacked on several more in Santa Fe. He doubted they'd be able to visit all of them in a day and a half. But that wouldn't deter him from trying.

Never having done anything like this, he asked, "Are you familiar with either city?"

"No," she replied. "I've never been here before."

"Help me understand why it's important to scope out a spot before shooting it."

She fiddled with her ear cuff. "In this case, the client doesn't want me to show up at a location sight unseen. Scouting helps with prep. I'll be able to visualize what might work best. For example, if the area is crowded with tourists, I'll need to know that in advance, especially if the client's production team can't clear them. Lighting is another issue. If the area is shaded, I'll have to light it myself."

"Understood."

If Zander had a knack for anything, it was charting a master plan, ticking off accomplishments, and moving to the next task. After reviewing each of the potential destinations and prioritizing them, he formulated a route using his phone's map app. In the twenty minutes they'd been sitting there, more than a dozen emails and text alerts had popped onto his screen.

"I'll wait while you handle those," she said.

"Absolutely not. I've got people covering for me so I can focus on you." Pausing, he stared into her eyes. "I'm all yours."

Her expression softened and the lines between her brows faded. "I'm concerned the quality of my work will suffer if I rush. I don't want the client to be disappointed. I always fear my current job will be my last."

Her vulnerability struck a chord. Though he wanted to press his palm to hers and offer a reassuring squeeze, he clutched his phone instead. "I will do everything possible to ensure you have a successful shoot."

And damn if she didn't reward him with a stunning smile.

Then, she stroked his arm. Perhaps her slow, gentle caress was meant to show her appreciation, but his body tensed with need.

"Thank you, Zander." She gave his triceps a little squeeze before letting go. "Oops, my bad."

"You're fine." *Damn fine.* He'd craved her from the moment they'd agreed never to touch each other again.

With a plan in place, they slid on their sunglasses and headed outside.

"How 'bout I drive?" he asked, while folding back the soft top on the Jeep.

"Have at it." She tossed him the keys and climbed in.

He jumped behind the wheel and started the engine.

"Let's rock this mountain city," she said.

Flashing her a smile, he cut into traffic.

Savannah plugged in her new phone. "Music helps me stay focused. Are you okay with that?"

"Of course. When I work, I get into what I call 'The Zone'. Years ago, I had to let an assistant go because he was too talkative. Even when working at his desk, he talked to himself, out loud, all day long."

She laughed. "Sounds like my mom. I would've done the same thing." She flipped on her playlist, and the provocative voice of an artist he didn't recognize crooned a sexy tune.

Savannah had closed her eyes, face tilted toward the sun, that swatch of dark hair buffeting her right eyebrow. *My God, she's beautiful.*

Being with his beguiling stepsister was proving to be more of a challenge than he'd expected. There was too much about her that he liked. She didn't force a conversation. In fact, she stayed focused on the job at hand and said very little. He admired her independence, yet appreciated how honest she'd been in sharing her concerns. Despite not winning the golf course job, she'd shaken it off and moved on. Her inner strength was as appealing as her physical beauty.

At the clothing store, she had plenty of opportunities to lay her hands on him, but she didn't. Instead of turning him around, she'd tell him to model the clothing. Rather than brushing her fingers over the cotton shirts he'd tried on, she asked him how he liked the feel of the material. He ached for her touch. Aside from that brief stroke of gratitude at the coffee shop, she'd adhered to their no-touch rule.

Damn.

As they drove to Petroglyph National Monument, he wanted to curl his hand around her thigh. At the traffic light, he gripped the steering wheel to keep from pulling her close and kissing her again and again. His fantasies made his pants snug in the crotch.

He stopped at the guard gate at Boca Negra Canyon, paid the attendant, and parked. A gentle breeze whispered past him and he inhaled the fresh air. He couldn't recall the last time he'd spent any time outside. "You ready to do this?"

"Let's check it out."

"You're the boss. Lead on." After exiting the vehicle, he slung both camera bags over his shoulder.

"We'll walk the Cliff Base Trail," she said, examining the brochure. "I can scope out the area, snap some test pics, and we can move on."

After hiking in silence for a few moments, Savannah stopped. She propped her sunglasses on her head and shielded her eyes from the bright glare. "This is perfect. That little shift in the clouds bathes the rock formations in bright white light. How beautiful."

Reverence filled her smoky voice. Sunlight hitting a bunch of old rocks didn't hold his attention, but Savannah did.

He set down her gear and she dropped to one knee, unzipped the bags, and retrieved two cameras, each with a different lens attached. While he should have been absorbing the natural surroundings, he couldn't take his eyes off her. Her soft expression, coupled with the joy in her eyes, captivated him.

With one camera slung around her neck, she started shooting with the other.

Click-click-click-click.

She stopped and examined the photos on the display, then moved to a different spot and continued shooting.

The park was filled with people, some with leashed dogs, others traveling the paved trail with large walking sticks. *Is this what people do on a weekend?* If Zander had been home, he'd be working, even on Saturday. He'd break to make a second pot of coffee. Might take someone to dinner. Steal an hour or two for sex, then return home and crash in bed, only to wake after a few hours, and begin again.

"I'm going to need you in a handful of the pictures," she said.

His eyebrows shot up. "Me? What for?"

"Models are provided on a lot of my shoots at the parks. You know, stick humans in the picture to encourage other humans to visit." She flashed him a smarmy grin. "You won't have to do anything. Just stand there. Can you handle that?"

"That, I can do. But posing will cost you extra."

SAVANNAH LIKED HAVING ZANDER by her side for more reasons than his business acumen, his keen organizational skills, and his dry wit. Her insides had heated with each outfit he tried on. By the time they left the clothing store, she'd been on fire.

The handsome, uptight suit had transformed into a sexy, rugged outdoorsman...wearing jeans that rode low on his hips and hugged those strong thighs. If she so much as peeked at his ass, their no-touch agreement would be null and void.

Turns out, agreeing *not* to touch him only made her more desperate to lay her hands on his rock-hard body or run her fingers through his hair and ruffle those slicked-down strands.

Another breeze cooled her sun-kissed cheeks and she faced

the wind. Being outside snapping pictures was her happy place. Being around Zander ignited something deep inside her heart that made her feel safe and secure—and less alone.

Stepping close, she tilted her face toward his. "Run your fingers through your hair."

He frowned. "What?"

"Mess it up. It's too neat."

"What difference does that make?"

"Are you arguing with me?"

He jammed his hand into his pocket. "Clearly. What does this have to do with being your assistant?"

"You're in my test shot and your slicked-down hair is catching the sunlight. It's distracting me."

"You do it."

Fighting against the desire, she dug her hand into her pocket. "No."

"What do you do on a shoot?"

"The stylist or makeup artist works with the models."

"And on the jobs when the budget can't afford them?"

She bit back a smile. "I do it."

"Have at it." He folded his arms across his muscled chest wall.

"No. I'm *not* touching you."

"If you don't do it, the pictures will suffer. You don't want that, do you?" As if trying to tempt her, he arched his brow and waited.

Desperate to feel his silky strands tickle her fingertips, she lifted her hand. Wasn't she breaking her own rule? She stilled, their fiery gazes locked on each other like two warriors doing battle. His breath shifted, his lids grew heavy. *He wants me to touch him.*

Desire thrummed through her. She wanted to throw her arms around him, press her lips to his, and kiss the hell out of him. Agreement be damned. Instead, she dropped her hand like a lead ball. "I'll manage."

"Dammit, Savannah." His jaw ticked as he raked his fingers through his plastered hair.

Her heart pounded a frenetic rhythm. Now, Zander King was flat-out gorgeous and totally irresistible. "Much better. You're very good at touching yourself."

He chuffed out a laugh. "Going forward, you should do it."

"Not happening, brother." Swallowing down the unrelenting lust, she backed up, lifted the camera, and began shooting.

Click-click-click-click-click-click.

She studied the test shots, then switched cameras. "Stay right there."

Retreating down the path, she chugged down a lung-filling breath. She'd never worked with anyone she wanted so badly.

Looking through the viewfinder, she scanned the area until she found her target.

Zander.

While waiting, he'd slipped one hand into the pocket of his jeans and extracted his phone. He stood, frozen, as if waging war with himself. Instead of checking messages, he shoved the device back into his pocket, and steeled his spine. *Nice.* Impressed by his willpower, she started snapping photos.

Click-click-click-click-click.

Not only did he ooze sex appeal, his rugged confidence shone through. *He's a beautiful man.*

A family walked into the frame, their laughter capturing his attention. The couple, with a toddler perched on the man's shoulders, stopped so the little boy could show Zander something in his tiny hands. When Zander graced her viewfinder with a smile, she zoomed in on his face. The man said something and Zander laughed.

Click-click-click-click.

Her heart swelled. That was the first time she'd heard him belly laugh. The couple chatted with Zander another moment before continuing on. When the little boy waved, glorious rays of sunlight illuminated Zander's face. But it was the unmistakable longing in his eyes that tugged at her.

Zander King might be an uptight suit, but beneath that protective armor was a man of flesh and blood...and heart.

Hers melted.

8

THE MASTER MANIPULATOR

A S ZANDER MADE HIS way toward his stepsister, her beauty stole his breath, her curvy body heated his, and her quiet strength brought peace to his troubled soul. He was in real trouble. Their no-touch rule wasn't going to hold up. Savannah Morrissette was impossible to resist.

As if she could feel his presence, she stopped studying the test shots and faced him. Her anxiety from earlier had been replaced with a sense of calm that radiated outward, like the sun's heat, warming everything in its path, including him.

"Do you spend any time outside?" she asked.

"Only when I'm at a construction site checking on a project."

"I love being at the beach or the mountains, a park or a ski slope. I'm always up for biking, hiking, even rafting. There's so much to appreciate about our planet by being out in it. My mom—you remember Debby—lived to gamble. If she wasn't dropping cash at a casino, she was betting at the racetrack. Her idea of spending time outside consisted of walking from the parking lot into the building." Though the climate was temperate, she shivered. While rubbing her arms, her smile fell away.

There it was. The *real* reason Savannah was against the Starry Cove Casino.

His stepmother, Debby King, loved to spend his father's money. Rarely home, she was all about buying designer clothing, handbags, and shoes, and less about her daughter. But his dad was too much in love with the flamboyant, flashy woman to mind her constant spending.

Before he could stop himself, he pressed his palms to her bare shoulders and caressed her soft, tanned skin. And the smoldering fire he couldn't tamp down burst into a flame.

Though soft, a whimper floated from her pouty lips. "You're. Touching. Me. Zander." Her crisp tone might have been meant as a scolding, but her body spoke the truth. Her lips parted and her brown eyes darkened with desire.

He should have stopped, should have stepped away, but he couldn't. Being around her, being by her side, wasn't enough. He needed to touch her. "I'm *comforting* you."

She stared up at him. "You shouldn't be."

"Who better than family?"

Her lips curved. "Naughty stepbrother." She knelt to tuck her cameras into their bags. When finished, she gazed up at him.

At the sight of her kneeling at his feet, an infusion of heat coursed through him. He envisioned her ultra-sexy mouth enveloping his cock. *Stop.*

She rose. "You ready?"

Beyond ready. He slung both camera bags over his shoulder. Touching her once wasn't enough. He wanted to haul her against him and keep her there.

On the way back to the car, she closed the space between them and, on occasion, her arm brushed against his. Zander's head spun from the contact. Why, if he couldn't have her, did he want her so damned badly?

He stored the equipment in the Jeep and climbed inside. "Sandia Peak is next."

She slid into the passenger seat beside him and shot him a little smile. He held her gaze before sailing out of the park.

"What kind of music do you like?" she asked.

"Classic rock, but I don't listen to much of anything these days. I grew up listening to the Rolling Stones, Queen, and—"

"Aerosmith," she interrupted.

"How'd you know?" He glanced in her direction.

"K-Dad listened to those bands all the time, especially on the weekends when he'd be in the shed tinkering with something."

Zander nodded. "I forgot about that. He'd stay out there for hours on Saturdays."

"He'd put on those paint-streaked coveralls and head out back. For lunch, I'd make him a sandwich and bring it out to him. I'd stay while he ate." Savannah brushed her bangs out of her eyes. "He gave me more attention than my mom did."

Again, Zander slid his gaze to her and held it for a beat before turning back to the road. "I'm glad he could do that for you."

"You must have hated me," she said and bowed her head.

"I resented my father, but I never hated you."

Her expression brightened. "How 'bout we listen to classic rock?"

"Sure."

After fiddling with her phone, Freddie Mercury belted out the time-tested lyrics of "Somebody to Love".

Zander didn't reflect on his childhood. But as they drove toward the mountains, he appreciated that he could share a piece of the past with someone who'd lived it right along with him.

Ten minutes later, they arrived at Sandia Peak Tramway. Like the pack mule he'd become, he grabbed her equipment, and they headed toward the station at the bottom of the mountain. After Savannah purchased tickets, they boarded the tram. The door closed, and they began their ascent.

The car was packed with people and Zander edged closer to

his stepsister to accommodate others. Her outdoorsy scent wafted in his direction and he breathed her in.

"This is breathtaking," she murmured as they climbed the mountain.

While the scenery was magnificent, he couldn't focus on anything but her. All he had to do was lower his head and kiss her shoulder or run his fingers along the top of her bare back and caress her skin. He could snake his arm around her waist and hold her against him, letting her supple curves meld with his hard ones.

She peeked up at him through her lashes. The air crackled with turbulent energy while he wrestled with his demons. He wanted to tell rational reasoning to go to hell and disregard the rule they'd set. He needed her in his bed, beneath him.

The tram locked into place, snapping him out of his salacious thoughts. After the attendant opened the door and the others scrambled out, Savannah heaved in a deep breath and exited the tram. Though he should have been relieved she'd put distance between them, he missed having her wedged up against him. She veered toward a vacant spot near the guardrail. As her dutiful assistant, he followed.

Five thousand feet below, the city of Albuquerque filled the landscape, the afternoon sun dipping towards the horizon. Temporarily freed from the daily grind, he gazed at the magnificent vista stretched out before them. And he took his first deep, cleansing breath in years. Grateful for this newfound sense of calm, he fixed his gaze on the one reason he was there.

Savannah.

She peered at the world through her camera. As he studied her profile, he wondered where life had taken her all these years. Other than what his father had willed them, and her profound love of nature, he knew close to nothing about her.

After taking several test shots, she lowered the camera and studied him. Her beauty and tranquility soothed his restless soul. *She should be in front of the camera, not behind it.*

"Beautiful view, don't you think?"

"It's perfect," she replied.

The spark in her eyes burned brightly. Her lips lifted on the corners, that sexy hint of a smile pulling him toward her. He wanted to get her alone, kiss her senseless, and tear off her clothes. Sex served his needs, but all he wanted to do was serve *hers*. Could she feel that constant tug? Her lips parted and she sucked in a harsh breath.

Yes, she could. For a man who followed every damn rule, he never imagined he'd willingly and adamantly want to veer from "right" toward "wrong".

But he did.

"Savannah." His voice strained against the desire he could no longer conceal.

She pushed up on her toes, pressed her lips against his ear. Heat streaked through him. "Let's go check out that hang glider."

With a smirk, she sauntered away, leaving him with a burgeoning boner and a host of fun, sexy ideas for how he could continue playing the role of dutiful assistant.

A guy strapped to a glider was perched on a large boulder, preparing for takeoff. When the glider launched, Zander's stomach dropped. Once away, the giant burgundy and gold wing sailed through the air, catching thermals and gaining altitude like a hawk.

Click-click-click-click.

"Guy's got balls," he muttered.

Savannah lowered the camera. "You could do that."

"Uh, no."

Zander would never sail off a mountain nor jump from a plane. His risks had always been career based, but, as the glider soared, he wondered what his life would look like if he did do something outside his comfort zone. He slid his gaze to Savannah. Being around her was freeing, exhilarating even. And her chill vibe was contagious.

A handful of tourists had stopped to watch her taking photos. When she lowered her camera, one of the men approached.

"Excuse me, are you Savannah Morrissette?"

When she smiled, his cheeks pinkened. "Sure am."

"I'm a huge fan. I met you at a San Francisco art show. You capture the serenity and grandness in nature better than anyone I've ever seen."

She placed her hand over her heart. "I appreciate your telling me that."

"Could I get a picture with you?"

"Of course."

Zander set down the bags. "Why don't I take the photo?"

"Hey, man, thanks." The guy handed Zander his phone. "Are you her assistant?"

Zander's massive ego ensured he played second to no one. But as he shifted his gaze to Savannah, he didn't need to prove his worth. "Yes, I am." Zander snapped a few pics and handed the guy his phone.

"I envy you," said the man. "You have a great job."

"I think so, too," Zander replied.

"Thanks for stopping," Savannah said.

Still grinning, the man rejoined his party.

"You're handling this assistant job better than I expected. Maybe I should add you to my payroll."

He stepped close. "I'm not interested in your money, Ms. Morrissette."

She held his gaze. "Hmm, how *will* I compensate you for your time?"

"You're creative. I'm sure you'll think of *something*."

She shook her head and shrugged. "Nothing comes to mind, Mr. King. Ah, wait, I know. I'll buy us some grub."

She snapped a few more test shots before they collected the gear and rode the tram back down. They squeezed in another scouting destination as a glorious sunset of fiery red, vibrant tangerine, and deep crimson popped against a plum sky. Having Zander by her side had calmed her down while riling her up at the same time. It was a heady combination that left her off-kilter and hungry for more.

On the ride toward Old Town, she spotted a restaurant with several bikers heading inside. "That looks like a local hangout. Wanna check it out?"

The neighborhood eatery was a large dive bar with a simple stage set up in the back. *This is great.* She wanted to kick off her shoes, toss back a beer, and listen to some good music. As Zander eased onto the wooden bench across the booth from her, she wondered if he'd ever hung out in a place like this. *Probably not. He's more of a white tablecloth and champagne kind of guy.*

Without bothering to open the menu, she asked the waiter to surprise her with a local draft beer and a popular fish dish.

The waiter grinned. "My kinda woman."

"That's my line," said Zander.

As they locked eyes, Savannah appreciated how the sun had turned his cheeks a rosy pink.

"You two are in luck," continued the waiter. "My favorite hometown band is playing tonight. They'll start in about an hour. Stay, if you can."

Zander ordered a Heineken and steak fajitas and the waiter buzzed off to fill their drink order. She wanted to reach across the table and unfasten the second button on his crinkled white shirt, but she didn't dare. Touching that man would open up a world of possibilities...all of them wicked good and super steamy.

After their beers were delivered, Savannah raised her glass. "To you, for saving my ass." She clinked Zander's bottle and guzzled. After draining half the ice-cold, golden ale, she set it down. "Ooeeee, that's good."

Her new phone chirped. Savannah pulled it from her back pocket and read the text from her mother.

"Where are you? Why haven't you returned MY calls!!! Did Kyle leave you any money????"

Savannah's stomach roiled. She set her phone face down on the table and swigged her beer.

"What's wrong?" he asked. "Something about the shoot?"

Her shoulders sagged and she sighed. "A text from my mom."

To her surprise, Zander smiled. His playful expression calmed her down. "She was…" He stared into Savannah's eyes for a few beats. "*Extreme*, but lively."

That made her laugh. "The 'Master Manipulator' is still on the hunt for her next wealthy victim. She's stuck in some decade where flashy and exorbitant reigned supreme. I made the mistake of telling her Kyle passed away and she's determined to find out if he left me anything."

"She'd self-combust if you told her we're using the land for a dog park and nature center."

Again, Savannah laughed. "If you tell her how you want to make Starry Cove a high-rollers paradise, she'll become your biggest advocate."

"What's her number?" he asked.

His playfulness was charming…and addictive. "I'm not sure her support is the kind you want."

"No, it's not," he agreed.

Despite the text, she didn't want to discuss her mother nor did she want to lose their chill vibe. He'd rested his hand on the table and she longed to run her fingers in the dips between his knuckles, then over the light dusting of dark hairs on the back of his hand. She flicked her gaze back into his eyes. "Thank you for today."

He downed some beer. "I'm the one who should be thanking you."

"Why is that?"

"First day in years I haven't worked. It's terrible timing with Kent in the hospital—"

She leaned forward. "What's that all about?"

"Do you remember Kent Walker from high school?"

"Sure. He was your best friend."

"He's my business partner."

"Is he okay?"

"He will be. He'd better be." Zander shifted on the bench. "He had a heart attack."

Before she could stop herself, she laid her hand on his. "I'm sorry to hear that."

He shifted his attention to her hand, then cocked an eyebrow. "Savannah." His word was meant as a warning she had no interest in heeding.

"Now, *I'm* comforting *you*." The air sizzled while they stared into each other's eyes. After a beat that lasted too long, she dragged her hand off his and clamped it around her glass. She ached to kiss him, run her fingers across his whiskered chin, and get lost in those amazing eyes. Instead, she sipped her ale.

He tossed back a mouthful of brew. "Turns out, being with you…er…I mean, being *outside* was the best thing I've done for myself in forever. I haven't taken a personal day since starting King Development. I came out here to change your mind about Starry Cove, and, now, discussing that project is the *last* thing I want to do."

The hair on the back of her neck prickled and she steeled her spine. She'd fully expected he'd want to discuss his project over dinner, especially after he'd spent the day helping her. *What's he up to? He looks sincere, but is he "pulling a Debby"?* Once again, her mother seeped into her thoughts.

When Savannah was a young child, the mayhem had begun at the grocery store when she'd been hungry.

"Here, eat this." Her mother handed her a banana.

"If I eat it, how will you pay for it?"
"Don't you worry about that. They expect people are going to snack while they shop."

Her mom had taught her to "take what you need" and things had spiraled downward from there. Savannah called her mother, the "Master Manipulator" for a reason.

As she drank her ale, she refused to allow her past to cloud her present. She would take Zander at face value until he proved her wrong. K-Dad had offered that valuable guiding principle.

"You've got my undivided attention," she said. "If not now, when? Monday's closing in. Why don't you tell me why this development is so important?"

The waiter swung by to tell them their dinners would be out shortly and suggested another round of beers.

Zander shifted his gaze to Savannah. "You in the mood for tequila?"

"Always." She eyed the waiter. "Two shots."

Zander covered her hand with his. Her heart skipped a beat while her skin heated from his touch. "How 'bout we do tequila my way?"

Her gaze flicked from his hand to his eyes. "Have at it."

"Do you have Herradura or 1800?" he asked the waiter.

"Herradura. Can I bring you those in a shot glass or a tumbler?"

"Tumbler," Zander said. "Make those a double-shot."

"And waters," she added.

"You got it." The waiter buzzed toward the bar.

To Savannah's surprise and disappointment, Zander removed his hand. Had he realized he'd been stroking her skin? Those small, gentle caresses had lit her insides on fire.

"STARRY COVE CAN WAIT a few more minutes," Zander said. "I haven't been this relaxed in a long time." Her beauty calmed him in some ways, excited him in all the ways that made him a man. "Tell me about you."

Savannah spent the next several minutes chatting about life, sticking mostly with her career. She was funny in a casual way, and he found himself smiling more than once. Maybe it was the alcohol. Could have been the comfortable clothes. No, it was Savannah. It was all Savannah.

"Granted, I've blocked out most of my childhood," Zander said, "but I don't remember you like this."

"I was shy. Internalized *everything*. Your dad helped me break out of my shell. In part, he gave me the attention I never got from my mom. Check that. I got attention from Debby, but it was all the wrong kind."

The waiter set down the tray with their top-shelf tequilas and ice waters. "Enjoy," he said before bolting off.

Zander raised his tequila glass. "Savannah, today was productive and fun. Helping you is exactly what I needed."

Lifting her glass, she toasted him. "The Stones say it best. 'You can't always get what you want'."

"Nicely put." He sipped the tequila, savoring the flavor before swallowing it down.

After tasting hers, she smiled. "*This* is tequila. You have great taste."

"Glad you like." He sipped again. "So, what did you mean by the *wrong* kind of attention?"

She regarded him for a few seconds, then brushed bangs off her brow. "Are you sure you want to hear this?"

He leaned forward, creating a more intimate environment. "I am."

"Between boyfriends, Debby had trouble keeping a job, so she taught me to shoplift."

He grimaced. "That's rough."

"She'd tell me all these insane reasons why not paying for something was okay. Lies masked in total bullshit, but I was too young to understand. It started with food when I was five, maybe six. Then, when she concluded I was good at that, she graduated me to clothes. Things got crazy when she had me stealing jewelry for her. I was afraid I'd get caught, but terrified of refusing her. She had a wicked temper."

What the hell? "I had no idea."

"Most of the money she did earn, she gambled away, hoping to make it big." Savannah rolled her eyes. "Life with Debby was one big soap opera of men, booze, gambling, and shoplifting."

"What a cluster fuck," he said, shaking his head.

Savannah chuckled. "Again, with the dry humor. I love it." Pausing, she grew pensive. "When she married your dad, and she got her hands on his money, she let up on me. It was a huge relief."

"Did my dad know?"

She shrugged. "Hard to know. I always wondered if that was the reason he was nice to me. You know…to balance out my mom." As she fiddled with her ear cuff, her fingers trembled. "After they split, she wanted me to swipe jewelry from a high-end department store while I was home from college. I refused, things got ugly. I bolted and never returned. That was the last time she tried to get me to steal, but the manipulation didn't stop."

A server delivered their plates of food.

His chest tightened at the abuse she'd endured. "There's more?"

"Yeah, but you've heard plenty."

"Please continue."

After a brief pause, she nodded. "When I started selling my photographs, and I had a little money, she'd call me with one sob story after another. Over the years, I've given her a bunch of cash, until I realized she was gambling it away."

"What a waste." Zander reached across the table and held her hand. He had to touch her, let her know he cared. "You're a good daughter, Savannah."

"Thanks, but Debby wouldn't see it that way. She was all about ignoring the rules or making up her own." She trembled and tugged her hand away to hug herself. "K-Dad helped me understand how rules are necessary and relevant. I learned respect rather than taking for personal gain." A sweet smile replaced her frown. "I've never talked about that, but I wanted you to know why your dad meant so much to me."

My God, she went through a lot. "Wow…that's…intense. I had no idea."

"I feel comfortable with you." She paused, their gazes cemented on each other. Then, as if she hadn't just bared her soul, she dug into her fish taco.

"Good choice?"

She held out the wrapped food. "Try it. You'll love it."

He suspected her devilish grin had nothing to do with the seafood and everything to do with what he shouldn't be considering—arousing thoughts he couldn't extinguish. The myriad of ways he could please her. All of them sexy and wrong. Very wrong.

After biting into the soft tortilla, he concluded he wasn't hungry for food. He was starving…for her. He wanted to wrap his arms around her, kiss her hard, and sink inside her. He started to harden. *This is going in the wrong direction.* He assembled his fajita and started eating.

He wanted to tell her the truth. He didn't give a damn about his father or their food, or even the alcohol. He didn't just *like* being around her—he craved her. From her beautiful smile and sultry voice, to how she shared her love of nature with him, he'd fallen under some kind of Savannah spell.

For the first time in what felt like forever, he would stop pushing to win. He'd savor *this* special moment with *this* amazing woman.

"Go on," he prodded after a few moments of silence. "Tell me about your relationship with my dad."

"This isn't too boring for you?" She scooped rice onto her fork.

He shot her a smile. "Listening to you is just what the doctor ordered," he said, and bit into his fajita.

He liked how her suntanned cheeks flushed pink. "I mentioned the camera he gave me for Christmas. In addition to encouraging me to take pictures of the other kids, he suggested I get outside and photograph the environment. That's when I developed my true passion. When you were at college, he took my mom and me to the beach for a week. He bought me several rolls of film, paid for the development, and went through each picture with me. My mom barely noticed. That sweet man framed and hung several photos around the house. He suggested I attend college, even helped pay for it. I got a degree in environmental science."

"He must've loved that."

Her lips curved. "He did."

Zander's father had been too busy chasing women or heaping attention on the ones he caught to offer his son the guidance and attention he'd craved. "You're more his child than I am."

"I don't know about that." Pausing, she drank some water. "I heard him talking to my mom about us. He told her he wasn't going to make the same mistake with me that he'd made with you. He wanted to do better with me."

The resentment that Zander wore as a protective suit of armor cracked. A small, tiny, fissure near his heart opened up a world of possibilities. His father had failed him, but he'd done better with his stepsister.

"He shaped my career, my ideals." She paused to eat. "He nurtured my love for undeveloped, untamed land. If that wasn't enough, he had integrity, something my mom desperately lacked."

"Where's your biological father?" He ate a forkful of rice.

"No clue. He was my mom's boyfriend until she told him she was pregnant. Then he was gone."

Their waiter popped over to check on them, giving them a natural break in the conversation. The relentless compulsion to check his phone every two minutes had faded into the background and he relaxed for the first time in over a decade.

"Okay, Zander, your turn." She wrapped her fingers around the glass of tequila and cemented her piercing gaze on his. "Tell me about your life before my mom and I barged in."

"Like you, I don't talk about my childhood or my relationship with my father."

She reached across the table, grasped his hand. "That's because we've never had anyone to talk to. This feels good, Zander. It feels right."

Is she talking about the cathartic conversation or the fact that she's holding my hand? He gazed into her eyes, alight with energy.

"I never set out to defy him." Zander sipped the tequila. "Had I known his passion for nature, I might have taken my career in a different direction. I sought Kyle's approval. Needed his attention. But I never got it. Don't get me wrong, it's good to know he gave you what he couldn't give me."

"Why'd he push you away?" she asked, before taking another sip.

"Looking back, I think he wanted to toughen me up. I was a clingy, insecure kid who eventually learned self-reliance, but I missed not having a relationship with him." He glanced at their clasped hands. Her fingers were long and soft. Her nails reflected a clear coat of shiny polish.

"I'm sorry he wasn't a better dad to you."

"Me, too." The more she caressed his fingers, the louder his blood whooshed in his ears. "We have more in common than I realized."

"Broken homes, but we turned out okay."

"You did," he said. "I'm still a work in progress."

Laughing, she pulled her hand away. While he appreciated her compassion, he sought something more, something taboo. He hungered to bring her the kind of pleasure no man should ever want to give his stepsister. Lusting after her was damned wrong. He shouldn't want her in his bed.

But he did.

He wanted her writhing beneath him and screaming his name when she surrendered to the carnal pleasures he needed to bring her.

"I've talked plenty," she said. "Tell me about King Development." Waiting, she cocked her head.

"It's okay. You don't have to..." He sipped more tequila.

"No, I mean it. I want to know."

He pushed his plate away. "Kent and I strove to create the area's most customer-centric commercial real estate development company. We started King Development right after college, worked twenty-four seven slogging through the small deals and building our portfolio." He smiled at the memory. "We had an absolute blast."

He explained why he wanted to develop Starry Cove and how the area would benefit from an infusion of business. He discussed a small portion of the financials, along with his long-term approach for the build-out.

"We want to hire as many of the townsfolk as possible and hope to lure back those who moved away. Our goal is to keep the small-town feel but offer modern amenities that will attract visitors. City or suburb dwellers who seek out that type of escape."

While Zander wasn't giving her a sales pitch, he watched for signs she'd lost interest or wanted him to stop talking. She'd leaned forward, tucked her hair behind her ear. Even if she never changed her mind, he appreciated that she was giving him her complete attention.

In those few moments, he made a decision. He wanted her to know the full story, even if it exposed a weakness. There was something special about Savannah that made it all right to bare his soul.

"I haven't been completely forthright." He set down his empty tumbler. "My business is in jeopardy."

"What's going on?" She handed her plate to a busboy who cleared the table.

Pushing his pride aside, he told her everything—from not winning forecasted new business to the large sum of money owed from an online university looking to build a brick and mortar campus.

"If things don't improve in the next thirty days, we're declaring bankruptcy. It won't be the end of King Development—just a financial reorg—but my employees are stressing over losing their jobs. I feel responsible to them, to their families." Breaking eye contact, he watched the band set up on stage. Telling her about his predicament reminded him that he could lose everything he'd worked for and all that he had.

She shook her head. "That's a lot of pressure."

"Spending time with you made me realize that no matter what happens, I've got to slow down. Make some life changes. Kent's right. I'm wound pretty tightly."

She grew quiet, gazing into her tequila like a fortune-teller deciphering the remaining leaves in a teacup. "I'll give your proposal serious thought," she said, breaking the silence. "We have until Monday to contact Sheldon."

Even though she hadn't changed her mind, the tightness in his chest loosened. He'd done everything he could and now he'd let it go. "No matter what you decide, I'll be okay."

Her sweet smile slayed him. "I like your new attitude, Zander."

So do I.

Savannah's phone vibrated on the rickety wooden table with an incoming call.

"Aren't you going to answer that?"

She glanced over and sighed. "It's my mother."

9

UNLEASHING THEIR NEED

"W HY DON'T *I* SPEAK to her? That'll give her a shock." Zander winked and flashed that wickedly handsome grin before sliding out of the booth. "Back in a minute."

Hoping she wasn't making a colossal mistake, Savannah answered. "Hey, Mom."

"I was worried sick over you. You didn't answer any of my texts or my calls. Where are you?"

When have you ever been concerned about me? "I'm working in New Mexico."

"How perfect! Time for a mother-daughter visit."

"Maybe when I finish up here."

"I can drive to you. It's a hop, skip and a jump from Vegas. Where in New Mexico are you?"

Per usual, Savannah regretted taking the call. "As much as I love twenty questions, I'm in the middle of—"

"Sooooo, I *know* K-Dad left you a shit-ton of money. Am I right? I'm right, aren't I?"

Her guts churned. "No money. He left me land intended for a nature conservancy that includes walking trails and a dog park." *Plus, he threw in a charming, historic inn and his Victorian home.*

"That stupid, selfish idiot." Debby grunted. "What good does a dog park do you? Can you flip it for some quick cash?"

"No. I can't get into this with you. I'm in a meeting."

"On a Saturday night? Don't you dare bullshit me. You're trying to get me off the phone. Look, Vanna, I'm low on cash. Spot me a few grand. You know I'm good for it."

Savannah's blood pressure spiked while her guts twisted into a painful knot. Those "loans" totaled over four thousand dollars. Just because she'd stopped doling out money didn't make these conversations any easier. "Do you need me to send you grocery store gift cards?"

Debby exhaled a sharp breath. "Never mind. Can you contest the will? Force someone's hand to sell the land? Cash is king, Vanna."

The waiter returned, saw Savannah on the phone, and started to leave.

"Hold on," she said to him. "Mom, I'm good with the will and I've *got* to run."

"Ah, the hell with you!" Her mother slammed down the receiver.

That went well. Rubbing her stomach, Savannah slid her gaze to the waiter.

"Can I bring you sopapillas?" he asked.

"Absolutely," she replied, fiddling with her ear cuff.

"Be right back with those," he said and left.

Zander slid into the booth. After a moment, his expression grew serious. "You okay?"

"All good."

"You want to talk about it?"

"I said I'm fine." But she wasn't. Even after all these years, her mother had the ability to rattle her.

"As your dutiful assistant, it's my job to ensure you remain in a good frame of mind." He clasped her hands in his and her defenses melted. "You're good when you're outside photographing nature. Or when you're kissing me."

She smiled. "I'm impressed. You've been paying attention."

He stopped stroking her fingers and removed his hands. Her heart dipped. "I keep everything bottled up," he said. "Never talk about anything. I can tell you from experience, it's gonna come out. For me, it's those damned headaches." He opened his palms, raised his brows. "If you can't trust your assistant, who can you trust?"

Her beautiful stepbrother had turned up the charm. Way, way up. She hoped his intentions were true. For a brief moment, she studied his face.

"Debby is tight on cash. I want to help her out if she's about to get evicted or she doesn't have any food." Savannah exhaled a sigh. "But she's all about buying something flashy or gambling it away."

"I understand. You question whether she's in a real bind or taking advantage of you. That's a tough spot to be in."

She appreciated his compassion. "It is. I offered to buy her grocery store gift cards, but she hung up on me." She shrugged a shoulder.

"You made a nice gesture, Savannah. That's all you can do. Most people have their own agendas. I know I did."

A shiver skirted down her spine. "And now what? You don't want to change my mind about Starry Cove?"

"No, I don't. All I ever do is push to win. I came here with that goal in mind." His gaze floated over her face. "One day didn't change me, but stepping away from the constant grind helped put things in perspective. Kent's heart attack has finally sunk in. I'm confident another opportunity will come along."

She liked this laid-back man who'd ditched the suit and had slowed down enough to be present and in the moment. The band started playing on the cozy stage behind her and she twisted around to see them.

"Come sit next to me," he said.

As soon as she slid in beside him, everything changed. His close proximity sent energy racing through her. His broad shoulders and hard chest filled the tight space. She soaked up his features, studied every detail. His dark, mussed hair made his light eyes pop. Those luscious lips were framed in a light sprinkling of facial hair. Eyeing his whiskered jawline had lust tumbling through her. But it was the intensity pouring from him that sent her pulse skyrocketing. Being around this sexy man was crazy addictive.

Beyond the handsome face and strong body was a man who'd walled himself off so he wouldn't get hurt. His vulnerability touched her soul. He used his suit as a protective armor, like she relied on the camera to shield her from others. Their porcupine exteriors made them more alike then she'd realized.

She understood him and longed to get closer.

While the slow beat of the music vibrated through her, she flicked her gaze from his mouth back into his eyes. She desperately wanted to kiss him. *Don't go there.* Refusing to give in, she severed their connection to check out the band.

The lead singer cranked out a tune with a southern rock beat. Zander dropped his arm on the back of the booth behind her, but he didn't touch her. She dug her heels into the floor to stop herself from nestling into the crook of his arm. *Resist, resist, resist.*

Despite closing her eyes and swaying to the slow, soulful beat, her thoughts stayed anchored on her stepbrother.

He was inches away, but she couldn't touch him. All she had to do was tilt her face toward him and he could kiss her. She set her sights on the band, refusing to surrender to the constant desire charging through her.

The song ended and the room broke out in applause and cheers.

"Savannah."

She peered into his eyes. Her heart pounded, her breath

caught. And her defenses crumbled. Damn this man. Damn his fiery energy, his brooding nature, and his sexy transformation.

"I can't hold back anymore. I have to kiss you."

Yes, finally. She moistened her lips. "If you must."

The corners of his lips quirked as their lips melded, desire surging through her. Her pulse quickened, her insides hummed. The kiss was soft, yet powerful. Bursting with passion and promise. She ran the pads of her fingers down his prickly cheeks. One soft peck blossomed into several, but his tongue never swept inside her mouth. She melted from the tenderness of his touch.

"Oh, guys, sorry to interrupt." Their waiter set down the plate of fried pastry. "Piping hot sopapillas."

Despite ending the kiss, Zander palmed her shoulder and pulled her flush against him. She struggled to steady her breathing. His gentle kisses had left her dizzy and starving for more.

"I brought you guys the works. Honey, along with our homemade sugar and cinnamon mix." He set everything on the table. "Isn't the band great?"

Savannah tried paying attention to the conversation between Zander and the friendly employee, but she couldn't. The hold her stepbrother had over her seemed surreal. She'd abided by their rule until he'd kissed her. And now, all she wanted to do was kiss him again.

Then, tear off his clothes and ravage the hell out of him.

They'd stepped into forbidden territory. Forbidden territory that would taste sweeter than the dessert she was about to devour.

When the waiter left, Zander murmured, "Now, where were we?"

"Being bad. We'd broken our no-touching rule."

He squeezed her shoulder. "We're still breaking it."

And that's when she realized she'd been caressing his thigh. Back and forth, up and down. Pent-up energy that had escaped without her conscious knowledge. She stilled her hand, but she couldn't remove it from his leg. Her willpower to resist this man had crumbled. "We. Are. Naughty."

His sinfully wicked grin made her tremble. "I could be if given the opportunity."

Heat blasted through her and she chugged her water, desperate for relief.

"Being with you has a dangerous, intoxicating effect on me," he said. "I haven't had a tension headache all day. For the moment, I'm not obsessing over work. But I am consumed with a constant desire to kiss you, like I'm possessed."

Breaking eye contact, Savannah doused the warm, doughy goodness in honey and offered him the dessert. "This'll cure you."

"I have a strong feeling this won't, but I know what will." Her insides tightened as he wrapped his hand around hers. As she slid the sugary pastry inside, she whimpered.

Their connection remained unwavering.

"You like?" she asked when he'd finished.

He nodded. "I like a lot."

Based on the searing look in his eyes, she suspected his answer had nothing whatsoever to do with the sopapilla.

"Do you like this?" She brushed her tongue over his lower lip before kissing him. "Mmm. So sweet."

"Jesus, Savannah, do you know what you're doing to me?"

"Not a clue," she said, peeking up at him.

Dipping his head, he kissed her. Electricity ran rampant through her sex-starved body. She couldn't stop trembling and she couldn't steady her breathing.

"How 'bout you?" he asked. "Honey or the sugar mixture?"

"I'll eat anything covered in honey."

"I'll remember that." He drizzled honey on the fluffy crust and held it out for her. "Come and get it."

"Why don't you put it in my mouth?"

His raspy moan made her panties wet. "Is that what you want?"

"Yes." When he slid the edge of the dessert into her mouth, she bit off a chunk. While she chewed, his gaze drilled into her, his eyes jet black with desire.

"More?"

"It's what I want, but it's not what I need." Leaning up, she kissed him, savoring his lips pressed to hers, his musky smell, and the promise of what they were going to do next.

His gritty groan sliced through the air and she anchored her hand on his thigh once again.

"What do you need, Savannah?"

"You," she murmured. "I need you."

"We shouldn't take this any further."

"No, we shouldn't," she replied. "But we will."

PASSION CONSUMED ZANDER. HIS stiff dick throbbed for the one person he should never desire. He wanted his stepsister and he was going to have her.

All of her.

As soon as he signed the credit card receipt, she slid toward the edge of the booth. "Thanks for dinner. I wish you hadn't paid."

"It was my pleasure." He'd become addicted to her smile.

"Ready to get out of here?" she asked.

"More than ready."

Once outside, Zander sucked down a lungful of cool, evening air. His insides were on fire. Savannah had unleashed something raw and primal he hadn't known existed. Tamping down on those overwhelming desires and emotions was taking all of his willpower.

"Thank you," he said, as they walked to the Jeep.

"For what? You paid for—"

Unable to stop himself, he threaded his arms around her, pulled her close, and kissed her. This time, he didn't hold back, and thrust his tongue into her mouth. He wanted to taste her, explore her, worship her. Her moan turned him harder still, but when she pressed herself flush against him, he deepened their embrace and tightened his hold.

The kiss continued, the intensity of their passion stealing his thoughts and consuming his ability to think clearly. He couldn't get enough of her. But he had to stop. Had to get a grip on his actions and wrangle his emotions under control. Panting, he slowed them down, dropped one more lingering kiss on her lips, before severing their fiery connection.

"Oh, my God." Breathing hard, she slid into the passenger seat.

As he walked around the vehicle, he exhaled a sharp breath before jumping in. He sat beside her, gazed into her eyes, but he had no words. Not a one.

She spoke. Her voice was hushed and he hung on her every syllable. And all she did was give him the name of her hotel, but her words floated in his head like a song he'd been waiting his entire life to hear.

He plugged the name into his map app and drove. The chilly air whizzed around them, cooling his overheated libido. Zander's hard-on had lasted for most of the evening. But he wasn't focused on relieving himself. He needed Savannah in ways he couldn't process. The tequila and the beer hadn't gone to his head, but the rush of being around this addictive woman had turned him into a drunken fool. He wanted her the way a tree needs sunshine, a dog needs human companionship, a living soul needs oxygen. And that scared the absolute fuck out of him.

Decades earlier, he'd forced himself to depend on no one, but the longing to pull her close, to touch her, to keep her by his side, would not go away. He'd hoped the alcohol would dull the ache. It had exacerbated it.

When he stopped at a light, he kept his eyes glued to the road and his hands cemented on the steering wheel. If he glanced in her direction, he'd pull over and take her on the side of the road, condom be damned.

And she deserved a hell of a lot more than that. She deserved his best.

He parked in the hotel lot. They each grabbed a camera bag and he slung his overnight bag over his shoulder before setting off toward the entrance. Logic and rules swam in a murky sea of brackish water.

"Tilly said I could crash in her room." That was his last, desperate attempt to squelch his taboo desires. To behave like a man with a moral compass and not one determined to bed his stepsister.

"Good idea."

His chest tightened. *Dammit.* He didn't like how quickly she'd agreed. But they were doing the right thing. Behaving like mature adults with common sense. They entered the building and she acknowledged the front desk clerk as they passed by.

"I have to check in," he said.

"Tilly's all checked in," she replied. "I took care of everything when I got here."

"So, you've got her room key?"

As she tapped the elevator button, her lips curved in a sly smile. "Sure do."

They entered, the doors closed, and she slid her gaze to his. He dropped his overnight bag, pinned her against the wall of the elevator and kissed her. Greedy and searching, their tongues thrust and tangled.

Bing.

The doors slid open, but he couldn't stop. The switch had been tripped, the need to be with her overpowering. She ended the kiss, nudged him back, and sauntered out as if that mind-blowing kiss had never happened. He collected his bag and followed.

Of course. Savannah and Tilly are rooming together. Energy surged through him.

She stopped in front of a door, dug out her keycard, and swiped it over the pad. "One room. Do you want to come in?"

Hell, yeah. "Yes." His voice didn't sound like his own. Every muscle, every nerve was coiled tight, desperate for that release. He pushed open the door and she sashayed past him.

"We're not behaving like a normal family," he murmured.

"That's because we aren't." Her snarky tone made him laugh.

When the door banged shut, the silence magnified his breathing. He deposited the bags on the suitcase rack. Then, he faced her. The atmosphere became charged. Once he started, he wasn't going to stop. And he needed confirmation she wanted this.

Her cheeks were pink, her lips moist. Like him, her breathing had become jagged. She'd cemented one hand on her hip while her eyes drilled into his.

"You are the one person I shouldn't want," he said. "And the *only* one I do."

"Sometimes being bad feels oh-so-good."

His sinfully sexy stepsister was so damned right.

MORE THAN A HOOKUP

"TAKE OFF YOUR CLOTHES." ZANDER'S husky voice dripped with control.

Unable to steady her breathing, Savannah swallowed down a moan. For a brief second, she hesitated. Had she even heard him correctly?

"Now or never, Savannah. Your call."

Inasmuch as she wanted to rip off her clothing and mount him, then take him inside her until she surrendered to the ecstasy, she needed *him* to strip her naked. She'd waited all day for him to touch every naked inch of her before he draped his body over hers and she took him inside. Finally, that wait was over.

"You do it."

His jaw tensed, his eyes narrowed. Two slow, deliberate steps and he stood close enough to touch her. His eyes were black with desire and locked on hers.

"We shouldn't." He untied her sweater from around her waist and it fell on the floor.

"I know."

"We can stop anytime." He gripped the hem of her tank, lifted the cotton shirt over her head, and dropped it on the sweater.

She shivered from the thrill pounding through her. "Right. Anytime." She couldn't get a handle on her breathing.

As he admired her breasts, a groan shot from his throat. The deliciously gritty sound ripped through her, landing between her legs. Cupping her breast over the black lace bra, he brushed his thumb over her hardened nipple. Adrenaline surged through her, the desire making her dizzy.

"Do you like what I'm doing to you?"

Closing her eyes, she leaned into his touch. She wanted this. She needed him. One night with this man would be worth whatever consequences she'd have to pay for her sins. "I love it."

Her eyes fluttered open when he nipped at her nib through the material. "You're super sexy," he murmured.

"Take it off me." Shivering from his delicious touch, she scraped her fingernails through his beautiful head of dark hair, eager to fist and pull on the strands.

Instead of attending to her other nipple, he cradled her neck with one hand while snaking his arm around her waist and hauling her flush against him. "It's all coming off, Savannah. All of it. You're not in a hurry, are you?"

"I'm dying for you, Zander." She toed off her shoes.

"Then, it'll be a sweeter release when it happens. I'm enjoying you. Your gorgeous face and sexy body. You don't want me to rush, do you?"

She was putty in his hands.

He unbuttoned and unzipped her jeans, then pulled them off her. Groaning, he stroked her ass, and cupped the small, hot space between her legs.

"You have a phenomenal body." As if admiring a piece of art, he turned her around.

He was deliberate, in complete control...and teasing the living hell out of her. *My God, he does sex right.*

After unhooking her bra and tossing it aside, he tugged down her thong. Then, he knelt and kissed her ass. Waves of lust washed over her.

"Turn around."

Pivoting, she stared down at him. The king of all things gazed up at her with a searing, greedy look in his eyes. "I want to eat you. Would you like that?"

Her knees trembled as she sank her fingers into his thick, dark hair. "Yes," she murmured. "Please."

Still kneeling at her feet, he kissed her tender flesh. She closed her eyes, shuddered in a breath, and widened her stance, clutching his hair for support. He kissed and licked while stroking her ass with one hand and anchoring his other around the back of her thigh.

His throaty groans sent white-hot pleasure streaking through her. One moment he was tender, the next forceful. With her teetering on the edge of a release, he slowed to a stop.

And then he rose. She stilled at the intensity emanating from his eyes.

"Kiss me," she rasped.

His perfect lips found hers and she pressed her naked body against his. Even through the denim, his thick shaft made her gasp. Their hot, open-mouthed kiss escalated into a frenzy of probing tongues and throaty moans.

The thrumming in her pussy made it difficult to think. She needed to kiss him, touch him, and feel his skin against hers.

Sinner on sinner.

"One of us has too many clothes on," she blurted between breaths.

"It would be too easy to lose control with you," he said while massaging and fondling her breast. "But you don't want a quickie, do you?"

Panting, she broke away. "I want you in as many ways and over as many hours as you can handle."

"I can handle a lot." He threw back the bed linens, toed off his boots, and yanked off his socks. "Lay down. I'm going to finish what I started."

"Not until you get naked."

"Once I'm undressed, I'm inside you. And I want to make you come first." He stepped close, grazed her erect nipple with the back of his finger. "You don't want to deny me that pleasure, do you?"

No, by God, she didn't. She slinked onto the bed and lay sideways. Pausing, he gazed at her naked form. A deep growl erupted from his throat as he yanked his shirt over his head.

She reveled in his hard, naked chest, those amazing abs, and his fabulous guns. Uptight suit had been hiding the goods, big time. "You're pretty damn hot, Zander."

"Baby, I've got nothing on you." Still wearing those sexy jeans, he planked over her. "My flamin' hot stepsister."

Loving the admiration he heaped on her, she whispered a thank you before he planted another kiss on her. His exploration continued with a trail of kisses down her neck to her collarbone. Taking his time, he fondled and kissed each breast, sucking and biting her engorged nipples.

When he ran his tongue over her hip, she flinched.

"I'm ticklish." She didn't recognize her own voice, coiled tight with desire.

Pinning her with a hard stare, he positioned himself between her legs. "Are you ticklish here, Savannah?"

"No." She swallowed, hard. "No, I'm not."

He pressed against her pink folds and licked her tender flesh. When he laved her opening and tongued her clit, she murmured, "I love that."

The more he licked, the more she gyrated. He swirled his tongue around her pearl and she ground against him. When he slipped two fingers inside her, she cried out.

She raised her arms onto the pillows, spread her legs, and started moaning his name. Her raspy sounds turned husky, her panting intensified, and she lifted her ass off the bed. With a gentle touch, he caressed her G-spot and she started shaking.

"Yesssss," she hissed.

A volcano of euphoria erupted from deep inside, the release sending streams of pleasure cascading through her. She continued shaking from the aftershocks until they subsided. Boneless, she opened her eyes and drank in the beautiful sight of him. Zander had fulfilled one of her favorite teenage fantasies and she loved every dirty second of it.

He dropped a worshipful peck on her sex before peering up at her with heavy eyelids, his face flushed with desire. Past hookups didn't include any kind of emotional connection, but this felt different.

He crawled up her, his expression a mixture of desire and cockiness. He was great at pleasuring her and he knew it. Damned if that didn't make her smile.

"Was that crazy good because *you're* good or because we shouldn't be doing this in the first place?"

"Oh, I'm good." He waggled his brows. "Very, very good."

She laughed, the high of being around him a thrilling rush. He kissed her before pushing off the bed. The bulge in his jeans reassured her they'd only just begun. After searching his overnight bag, he shook his head. "Dammit. I don't have a condom."

Rising, she sashayed over and rummaged through her camera bag. After finding one, she sauntered close. "Let the party continue."

"You are one wild woman."

She trailed her fingers over his shoulder and down his arm. "I'm not as wild as you might think, but I don't want to ruin your impression of me." She pushed up on her toes and kissed him, their connection setting off a series of mini sparks.

He stroked the sides of her body, up and down. "*This* is wild."

She caressed his pecs, her fingers whisking over his chest hair, setting every nerve on fire. "*This* is rocking hot sex with someone we once considered family." Leaning in, she dotted his skin with kisses. With each one, her insides came alive.

"You feel damn good," he said, running his hands along her back. "I've been fantasizing about you all day."

She slid her gaze to his. "Naughty stepbrother."

"Temptress stepsister."

She smiled. "That I am. *Now*, can we get you naked?"

"Yes, ma'am, and you can take full advantage of me, too." The cadence of his voice was slow and deliberate. The tension around his eyes had been replaced with a gleam. Uptight suit was long gone. A gorgeous, hunk of a man towered over her. One with hard muscles and mussed hair, who'd just given her permission to ravage him.

And ravage him she would.

"It'll be my pleasure." She tugged off his jeans and relieved him of his boxers. Before laying hands on him, she stepped back and gripped her hips. As she gave him the once-over, heat blanketed her body. This was no ordinary man. This was an Adonis. "My God, you are the total package."

Feeling heady, she took a step forward and grasped his jutting cock with both hands, caressing the shaft and smooth head. A breathy moan escaped his lips while he anchored his hand on her shoulder.

Instead of closing his eyes and reveling in the pleasure, he peered into hers. Intensity rolled off him in waves. *He's beautiful.* She didn't need her camera to see that.

Cradling her chin in his other hand, he tilted her face toward his. Then, he dipped down and kissed her. Her heart hammered, her breath hitched. She tightened her hold around his shaft while sliding her other hand around his ass and stroking his warm skin.

Her breath came in short gasps or she forgot to breathe at all.

She took the smallest step toward the bed and he was right there with her, moving as one. He slithered his arm around her waist, easing her onto the mattress. This time, when he kissed her, they came together in a clash of lips and tongues. She inhaled his hiss and reveled in the sensual way he touched her. His fingers roamed over her as if he was committing the curves and nuances of her body to memory. She couldn't get enough of him. Didn't need anything but him, buried inside her. Her insides throbbed, her body primed to take him.

Panting, she ended the kiss. "I can't wait any longer, Zander. Please, *please.*"

The desperation in her voice curved his lips. She swatted his muscled shoulder as he moved off her, tore open the condom packet, and covered himself. Then, he hovered over her, his arms pressed to the mattress, trapping her.

Being with him freed her and terrified her all at the same time. These intense feels shouldn't be happening with *this* man.

He didn't enter her. Instead, he kissed the swell of each breast, taking his time to pamper her with doting touches and gentle kisses. When he clenched her nipple with his teeth, desire surged through her. Gazing down, she watched the deft way he kissed, sucked, and laved her erect peaks. Already engorged, they doubled in size as he savored them with his talented mouth.

She wanted to speak, to tell him how good he felt, but the words stuck in her throat. As if he could sense her struggle, he stopped and shifted his gaze to hers.

"Do you like?" he asked.

"So much," she rasped out.

He repositioned himself at her opening, but he didn't push inside. She quivered from the torture of his denying her.

"I want you in a way that makes me crazy," he said. "I shouldn't want you this badly, but I do. As much as I don't want to say this, if you asked me to stop, I would understand."

She smirked, sucked down a lungful of air, and arched toward his hardness. "I'm on fire. Please, I'm begging you. I know this is wrong, but I must have you."

As he pushed inside, she cried out from the exhilaration of their connection. He covered her mouth with his. The kiss turned incendiary, their moans interspersed with short gasps while he worked his way inside her.

"Yes," she murmured between kisses.

"I need you, Savannah."

The rawness of his words stilled her. She needed him, too. *No, this is sex. Nothing more.*

When he started moving inside her, she matched him, thrust for thrust.

"Look at me." She'd spoken the words before she could filter them.

He did. And then he stopped moving. "You're an amazing woman, Savannah. Beautiful. Sensual. And fun." Soft, intimate words spoken between two lovers.

But romance wasn't supposed to be on the menu. Raw and unfiltered intercourse was. She'd wanted this to be screwing without emotion until he'd spoken those words. The ones that touched her soul and melted her from the inside out.

She could have uttered those same words, but like earlier, they lodged in her throat. She whispered her appreciation before shifting so he could sink in farther. Then, she threw her leg over his ass, raised one arm over her head, and arched toward him. "Kiss me."

Their lips met, their lustful dance only heightened by his powerful words. The sweet aroma of sex hung in the air while he moved inside her again. Closing her eyes, she rode the exhilaration. The high of being with someone she'd fantasized about for years overtook her and she reveled in the hunger of his kiss and the slow, sensual way his tongue tangled with hers. She gripped his biceps and hung on while his heavy breathing thundered in her ears.

Overtaken with euphoria, she increased her speed, while he plunged deeper and faster. She swallowed his throaty moans during another searing kiss and, when he told her he was going to come, she let go.

Shaking through her orgasm, she clasped her arms and legs around him, while he poured himself into her.

Wrong shouldn't feel so damned right.

THE SURPRISE

Z ANDER'S EYES FLUTTERED OPEN in the dimly lit room. He'd been dreaming that his sexy stepsister was sucking him and he was reveling in the pleasure. When the sensation continued and Savannah's guttural groans hijacked his attention, he realized his cock was in her mouth.

"Holy hell."

Her full lips were locked around his shaft and he gritted his teeth and moaned as she sunk down farther.

She cupped his balls in her hand and massaged them. Pure euphoria emanated from every crevice of his body and he rose on his elbows to watch how she teased with her tongue before taking him into her mouth again.

When she slid her hand beneath his ass and caressed his anus, he flinched. "Oh, wow."

She pulled off him. "You like?"

"I don't know...*yet*."

Her smarmy grin made him smile. "I'm not going inside, but if it's not your thing, tell me and I'll stop."

"I must be dreaming."

With her fiery gaze cemented on his, she swirled her tongue

around the rim of his cock and eased him back inside. She lashed her tongue over the head and rubbed the tender spot under it. His dick grew rock hard and he dropped his head on the pillow, closed his eyes, and appreciated her incredible and generous talents.

This time when she stroked the outside of his anus, he relaxed into the exciting new sensations. "That feels good."

Her deep throating ratcheted up the ecstasy overtaking him. On a groan, he reached down and sunk his hands into her wavy hair. She continued working the head of his cock while she gently rubbed his tender back end.

The orgasm started deep inside, teasing and pleasing until it burst out of him with such force, he jerked violently on the bed. She sank onto him and groaned while he released himself into her.

A moment passed before he could think. And another before he could speak. "Savannah," he murmured.

She crawled up like a tigress and kissed him with such passion, he wondered how in the hell he was ever going to let her go.

"You're amazing."

She lay down beside him. "I can't control myself around you."

He knew exactly how she felt.

Despite not being a cuddler, he scooted down, laid his head on her stomach, and stroked her thigh. Her gentle fingers played in his mussed hair and she caressed his back. Moments passed with nothing but tender touching. They'd created a special space where words weren't necessary.

He snuggled up beside her and she spooned into him. He kissed her soft shoulder and caressed her breasts, her stomach. He loved exploring her body, feeling her silky skin beneath his fingertips.

He stroked her clit, slipped his fingers inside her folds, and she repositioned to give him easier access.

"Mmm, that feels nice. I like how you start slowly and build."

"You're so sexy, so wet."

He rubbed and teased, taking his time to listen to her breathing, feeling her body tense against him. He kissed her back, nibbled her shoulder. He inhaled her beautiful scent. A mixture of sex, Savannah, and a lingering hint of the outdoors.

He took her to the edge, slowed back down, then revved her up again. Her soft whimpers grew to hoarse cries.

Craning her neck, she murmured, "Kiss me."

When he did, she let go, shaking and shuddering in his arms.

In the afterglow, she rolled towards him and snuggled against his chest. He wrapped her in his arms and kissed the top of her head. As they lay together, contentment settled over him. He'd no idea how to process this foreign feeling, let alone communicate it. His happiness went beyond the physical high of sex and fell outside the realm of lust, too.

He liked Savannah, respected her, craved being near her. He'd flown to New Mexico to change her mind. In one day, she'd softened his hardened heart.

Does she realize the effect she's having on me?

"I really like you," she whispered.

"I like you, too."

He nestled closer, grateful they had one more day together. His breathing fell in line with hers and, as he drifted off, he couldn't remember ever having fallen asleep holding someone so close to his heart.

EARLY THE FOLLOWING MORNING, Savannah rolled over to find the other half of the bed empty and her very hot "assistant" missing. Last night's clothing lay neatly on the bureau. That small act of thoughtfulness made her smile, but, as she pushed out of bed, her chest tightened.

When she didn't find Zander in the bathroom, she was grateful for a moment alone. After brushing her teeth, she stepped into the shower.

As she'd suspected, the sex had been phenomenal. Unlike her rule-abiding stepbrother, her issue didn't revolve around their familial connection. They might have been a blended family at one point, but they weren't blood-related.

Savannah's real fear? Intimacy.

Hoping to relieve her anxiety, she stood beneath the hot spray and let the water pound her shoulders.

Had she hooked up with someone else, she wouldn't have invited him to stick around long enough to cuddle. This time, however, she couldn't duck out. The unresolved issues in Starry Cove had to be handled. Even if she did nothing about the undeveloped land, they still co-owned an inn and K-Dad's home. And, so far, they'd agreed on nothing.

For the first time, she'd crossed the line and mixed business with pleasure. *Just don't do it again.*

She toweled off and left the bathroom. Still, no Zander. She checked her phone.

"Grabbing us breakfast," he'd texted.

Her heart bloomed at his kindness.

Beyond their intense physical attraction, she was drawn to his quiet strength. His vulnerability struck a chord with her, too. His company had run up against tough times, something she could relate to.

Having him with her made all the difference, logistically and personally. Going it alone these past several months had been more of a challenge than she'd realized.

They'd had one night—one fantastic night—but that was the beginning and the end of their fiery connection. Her heart squeezed. There was something special about Zander that tugged at her soul.

After pulling on jeans and a shirt, she reviewed the previous day's test shots. Zander had made all the difference. The pictures were good, but her frame of mind was even better. Without his help, location hunting would have turned her into a frazzled wreck.

Knock-knock-knock.

Camera still in hand, she opened the door and her brain shorted.

"Oh, for goodness sakes, Vanna, don't stand there gaping at me," said her mother. "Invite me in."

"Mom, what the—?"

A whoosh of vibrant pink, neon green, and bold orange barged through. Debby King's jet-black hair had been teased into a poufed updo and she'd caked on a thick layer of makeup. As the door banged shut, Savannah sneezed from the heavy dose of perfume.

"Yes, yes, I know you're surprised to see me." Eyeing the room, her mother grimaced. "This is blasé, but never mind that. Your dim-witted manager explained how you're running around the city half-cocked. I had to rearrange my mani-pedi, my girls' luncheon, and a shopping excursion with my new honey pie. But your mama's here to help."

Backing away from the whirlwind of energy, Savannah clutched the camera to her chest. "If you talked to Tilly, you know I'm under a crazy deadline. What are you *really* doing here?"

"Helping you formulate a plan, of course." Debby hitched her hands on her hips. "If Kyle King left you anything, we've got to sell it…and lickety-split. You'll finally be able to quit all this silly picture-taking nonsense." She sauntered close and Savannah whiffed the stench of cigarettes. "Your mama's caught herself a deliciously adorable boy toy—oh, you'd love him, Vanna. He told me he's going to win big at craps."

Savannah felt like crapping. "Look, Mom, you've got to go."

"I did not just drive all night for you to dismiss—"

The door swung open and Zander entered carrying a cardboard tray with two covered drinks and a white paper bag.

He flicked his gaze from Savannah to Debby and his smile dropped like a lead ball crashing onto the pavement.

Debby swirled around, the kaleidoscope of colors in her mother's flashy pants suit and matching cape nauseating Savannah.

"Good God, Vanna, you've got a man in your room."

Debby King was a master at stating the obvious.

"Hello, doll baby. Ooo-o-o, you're a *hottie*." Debby winked, then nibbled her lip before flicking her gaze back to Savannah.

After Zander set the tray on the table, he handed a cup to Savannah. "Good morning." He shot her a smile.

This isn't good. Swallowing down the bitter taste of bile, Savannah accepted the hot drink. She had no words. A scream scratched and clawed at her throat, but she kept her mouth clamped shut.

"Black coffee," he continued, as if the tornado known as Debby King hadn't blown into their hotel room. Then, he shifted his sights to his former stepmother and the warmth in his eyes turned to steel. "Hello, Debby. It's been a while."

Her mother's mouth fell open. Savannah hoped a fly would zoom in.

"Well, fuck me," Debby blurted.

Savannah cringed at her mother's foul language.

"No, thanks. I'll pass," he replied stone-faced.

"Well, if it isn't my stepson, Zander King." She examined him from head to foot. "Here to steal Savannah's inheritance?"

Ironic coming from the queen of shoplifting.

"You're looking...festive." His stoic expression gave nothing away.

Her mother raised her chin, crossed her arms, and narrowed her gaze. Debby's fighting stance. Then, her lips split into a terrifying smile. "Festive is my middle name. So, Zander, do you live in the area? Did you drop in to offer Savannah a tasty pastry in exchange for Kyle's money?"

Zander's jaw ticked. "Is that why you're here?"

"Me? I'm here to help my daughter, of course." Her plastic smile sent a shiver streaking down Savannah's spine. "Her worthless ditz of a manager told me she's working her tail to the bone, poor baby."

Savannah set her coffee on the small desk. "Tilly's right. I am working and won't get into a discussion about Kyle's will." Despite her pounding heart, she kept her voice low and steady. Debby King might know how to push all her buttons, but Savannah wasn't going to give her the satisfaction of knowing that.

As if everything was good and right and normal, Zander pulled out a handful of pastries and set them on the paper bag. "Help yourself, Debby. Have you had any coffee today?"

She uncrossed her arms. "I did."

He pointed to a pastry, but Debby declined. "Savannah, what would you like?"

Savannah waved him off. "No. I'm fine."

"We've got a big day ahead of us. I'd suggest you eat something." He handed her a blueberry muffin. "The woman at the bakery said these were fresh out of the oven." His carefree smile made her want to shriek. How could he remain calm and why wasn't he kicking her mother out of their room?

After taking the muffin, she set down her camera and broke off a small piece. Though she'd lost her appetite, she popped the morsel into her mouth. She had to do something besides gape.

"I reviewed the locations in Albuquerque that we didn't hit yesterday and think we'd be smart to head to Santa Fe first, then drive back down here and knock those out," Zander continued as if her mother wasn't eyeing him with complete disdain. "We might want to move faster today, but I don't want you to feel rushed."

His even-keeled voice helped slow her palpitating heart.

"I'm ready to get going," she replied, shooting daggers at her mother, hoping she'd take the hint and leave.

Debby smacked her hands together and Savannah flinched. "I don't like the looks of this. You two are working together?"

"We are," Zander replied matter-of-factly. "I'm her assistant."

Debby's shrill laugh made Savannah jump again. "That's a load of bullshit. You're trying to swindle my little girl." She launched her cherry red fingernail in Zander's face. "Let me tell you something, buster. I taught my daughter to trust no one. She's not stupid enough to fall for your swagger and your hot-shot looks."

Savannah pushed past them both and yanked open the door. "Get out." She glared at Debby. "Out. You have no business—"

"Shut up, Vanna. Zander is a big boy and..." Pausing, Debby flicked her gaze from the made bed to the unmade one. "Jesus, are you two screwing? What kind of perverted kink are you into? Who fucks their family?"

As Savannah closed the door, acid churned in her stomach.

Crossing his arms over his massive chest, Zander faced Debby full-on. "What your daughter and I do or don't do is none of your business."

Her mother glared at Savannah. "I taught you to be smarter than this. Who in their right mind sleeps with their stepbrother? Are you insane or just plain desperate? Some hunky guy with a foot-long hotdog comes along, offers you a little *help*," she inserted air quotes for emphasis, "and you go all soft?"

Savannah couldn't argue. Zander did want her to change her mind about Starry Cove. Just because her mother was a loose cannon, didn't make her wrong.

"Debby," Zander said. "I don't care how you speak to me. But do not talk to Savannah like that."

"Piss off, Zander. All you care about is taking advantage of a sweet, grieving woman who has a blind spot when it comes to Kyle. In her eyes, he could do no wrong." She fiddled with the string of bracelets on her wrist. "You weren't the only one who didn't get his attention."

What the hell? Savannah flicked her gaze from one to the other.

"Because of Kyle and his cockamamie, illogical reasoning, Savannah is obsessed with protecting the land." Debby gave him the once over. "And what do *you* do for a living?"

"I'm a developer."

"Of what?"

"Land."

She rolled her eyes. "My God, Vanna. He's playing you. Can't you see that?"

The poison Debby spewed made Savannah's stomach roil. "That's enough—both of you." She had a lot of ground to cover in a short amount of time, not to mention getting her head back in the game. If there was anything Debby was good at, it was messing with her psyche. "Time for me to go."

Savannah set the uneaten muffin on a napkin and grabbed the keys to the Jeep.

Debby yanked crumpled papers from her hot pink, polka-dotted, designer handbag and waved them in the air. "As Kyle's will states, I'm the only one listed as his beneficiary. He left me everything. So, what do you have to say to that?"

"That's an outdated will." Zander sipped his coffee.

"How do you know?"

"The one my dad's lawyer gave us is dated this year. Is yours?"

"I'm contesting your will...er...um, I mean, *alleged* will," Debby bleated out.

Pausing, Zander sipped his coffee again. Savannah marveled at how in control and calm he appeared.

"You're going to waste money on an attorney that you could be spending on more important items, like clothes or playing the slots," he said. "Are you prepared to throw that cash away?"

"I was his wife and should be included." Debby rummaged through her tote bag, unearthed a gum packet, and popped a stick into her mouth.

"But you aren't," Zander said. "None of his exes are named, which will hurt your chances of winning. And you're all about playing the odds, aren't you? The money he left is tied to a dog park, walking trails, and a nature conservancy."

The fire in her eyes went out and her upper lip curled. "Vanna can contest that."

Zander glanced at his watch. "Debby, I'm going to do us all a favor. This is a first for me, but I'm going to make you a deal you won't want to refuse."

"How delightful. I love deals." She gnashed the gum like she was working a piece of beef jerky.

He leaned against the small bureau. "How's five thousand dollars sound?"

Her eyes lit up. "It has a nice ring to it. Why?"

"That's how much I'll give you to stop badgering Savannah for money and not contest Kyle's will."

After admiring her long, manicured fingernails, she addressed Zander. "As tempting as a monetary gift would be, five thousand is an insult. Kyle King was a wealthy son of a bitch back then and he probably died just as stinking rich."

"That money wouldn't come from Kyle's estate," Zander said. "I'm offering you *my* money."

Her plucked eyebrow arched. "Hmm, so you want me to take the money and run?"

"Yes."

"You can't buy me off. I'm not a gnat you can swat away." She pivoted toward Savannah. "I came here to talk some sense into you and to help you out because your manager—"

"Tilly's my agent."

"Whatever the hell she is, she isn't doing her job. You are easily taken advantage of, Vanna, and that pisses me off!" Angry, beady eyes launched daggers in Zander's direction. "Don't be a fool, Savannah. I can protect you from men like this who prey on unassuming women like you."

Hoping for a little relief, Savannah rubbed the back of her neck, but the muscles had hardened to stone. "When have you *ever* protected me?"

"If you make Kyle's money work for *you*, you can spend the rest of your life snapping beautiful pictures of your forever happy places. You live in a dream world, my sweet girl. Wake up and see this man for what he really is. Life is hard. You've got to work the system or it'll work you...to *death*."

Savannah had endured enough. "As much as this makes me sick to my stomach to say, I want you to take Zander's offer and leave. I love my life. I love taking photographs, and I'm ecstatic that I'm no longer under your thumb. I don't care about *things* because I never got any joy from stealing for you. I got stomachaches and a messed-up perspective of how the world works." Her skin crawled with what felt like a thousand centipedes.

"Very well, if you insist." She addressed Zander. "Do you have your checkbook with you?"

He handed her the hotel notepad and pen. "Give me your contact information. My attorney will email you an agreement."

As Debby scribbled her information, she asked what the agreement would include.

"You don't contest the will and you stop harassing Savannah for money."

"No problem. When can I expect the money?"

"Next week."

"Lovely doing business with you, Zander." She flicked her gaze toward her daughter. "I hope you figure out how the world works before this land developer takes complete advantage of you. And get yourself a new agent!"

And with that, Debby King and her kaleidoscope of shocking colors sailed out of the room.

When the door banged shut, Savannah's knees gave out and she crumpled into the chair.

ON THE ROAD AGAIN

ZANDER FEARED HE'D DONE more harm than good by offering to pay off his former stepmother. Savannah's lips were slashed in a thin line and she refused to look at him. Her silence sent a chill down his spine.

"I'm sorry," he said, sitting on the edge of the bed closest to her.

More silence, until she flicked her laser gaze in his direction. "Now that you've thrown money at Debby to make her go away, she's going to attach herself like an octopus. Once she wraps her tentacles around you, you're trapped." When Savannah raked her hand through her hair, her fingers trembled.

Zander's heart broke for the turmoil brought on by her mother...and by him. Leaning toward her, he cupped his hands over hers. "I can handle her. I couldn't stand listening to her berate you. When we were kids, I kept my interactions with her to a minimum..." His voice trailed off. "Until yesterday, I had no idea she was that venomous."

"I think it would be best if you didn't join me today." The pain in her eyes pierced his heart.

But she hadn't pulled her hands away, so he stroked her soft skin with his thumb, and he waited. There was no way in hell he was leaving her, not after that fiasco. "I promised Tilly I'd assist you and I'm a man of my word. I had a great time yesterday and I'm looking forward to exploring Santa Fe with you. Let's not let Debby ruin our day. Please, Savannah."

Zander never begged. He was begging now.

While she studied his face, her expression softened.

He pushed off the bed, leaned against the bureau. "I've been honest with you from the get-go. I came here to change your mind, but I've put aside my agenda to help you. You know I don't want a dog park. I want to renovate that…that…what the hell did I call that place?"

"The Town that Time Forgot." She cracked a small smile and his pounding heartbeat slowed.

"Yesterday was great," he continued, determined to make things right between them. "But last night was pretty damn special."

Her shoulders relaxed and the creases around her eyes faded away.

"I didn't use you, Savannah, and I'm not using you now." He held out her muffin. To his surprise, she took it and tore off another piece.

He wanted to wrap his arms around her and tell her that yesterday was an amazing day because *she* made every moment special. He ached to kiss every inch of her face until her sadness melted away and her melodic laughter filled his ears. He could see the pain in her eyes and he wanted to replace it with joy. He wasn't proud of what he'd done by paying Debby off, but he had to do something—*anything*—to protect Savannah.

Instead, he said, "This isn't how I'd envisioned our day would start."

She closed her eyes, inhaled deeply, then opened them. "Me, either."

"I offered to pay her off for you. If she stops pestering you for money, maybe you two can have a real relationship."

Savannah barked out a laugh. "I think the sun has baked your brain. She doesn't want a relationship. She wants things. She wants to manipulate me. She wants me to quit my dream job or, better yet, become her professional thief."

Jesus, that's insane.

His fingers tingled to pull her close, but he stayed anchored to the bureau. "Just because she doesn't find value in your career doesn't mean a thing. You found your happy. Your art brings joy to others, like that man at Sandia Peak." He smiled. "And me."

When her eyes brightened, the tight muscles running down his back released.

"If she contests the will, it'll be tied up for months," he continued. "Sheldon would be placed on retainer and nothing would happen anytime soon. I'd rather have a damn dog park and butterfly garden than get into it with my former stepmother. And from what I can gather, you have too much going on with your own career to deal with that." He eyed the time. "Please don't send me away. We have a big day ahead of us and I'm eager to get back outside and work on my tan."

As she slung her handbag over her shoulder, he caught her smile. Relief coursed through him.

"A butterfly garden, huh?"

"Well, we've got to put something worth seeing in that nature center." He shouldered both camera bags and they left.

In the parking lot, he had to touch her, make sure she'd stopped shaking. He slung his arm over her shoulder. Her trembling had stopped. When she didn't pull away, he kissed the top of her head, inhaling her beautiful scent while his heart rate slowed back down to normal.

They jumped in the vehicle and he headed north. After weaving his way out of the city and jumping on I-25, he let the

Debby fiasco fade with the Albuquerque skyline in the rear window. Ready to start afresh, he broke the silence.

"I mapped out the spots in Santa Fe." He handed her his phone. "Do these work for you?"

Pulling her phone out of her handbag, she checked her client's email. "Santa Fe Botanical Garden, Wetland Preserve, The Plaza, and Bandelier National Monument. You've got 'em. Thanks for taking care of this."

"Feel any better?"

"Not really, but I've stopped shaking." She held out a steady hand.

"I'd forgotten what a ball of energy Debby is."

"More like a cyclone."

He chuckled. "Do you accept my apology?"

"Of course I do," she replied. "Thank you for having my back. No one has stood up to her like that."

"Are we good?" *Please say yes.* On impulse, he stroked her leg. Had to touch her again.

"We should probably talk about last night."

His chest squeezed. *Dammit. Here it comes.*

She slid on her sunglasses. "What we did was wrong."

"Very wrong." *But it felt so damn right. Come on, Savannah, gimme something good.*

"I...um." She paused, shifted in her seat. "I'm not sure...I mean...we—you and me. We had a good time. It's just that we'll be working together on the inn...and the land. You know what they say about mixing business with pleasure. I'm thinking we should keep things chill."

Ah, hell. At the moment, he didn't give a damn what "they say". But he did care about her thoughts and feelings. Shoving aside his bruised ego, he removed his hand from her thigh. "Right. Of course."

At least he knew where he stood with her. *Gotta hand it to my stepsister. She doesn't leave a guy hanging, that's for sure.* He'd been an idiot for thinking this could turn into something. They'd had a few drinks. Gotten caught up in the moment. Two consenting adults having a good time. She'd been an escape from reality, nothing more.

That's total bullshit.

He wanted to challenge her. Confront her. He'd spent his entire life following all the damn rules. Rules were designed for a reason, but he'd tossed those out the window when it came to Savannah.

He knew how easily she could undo him with her smile. Or the way her eyes lit up when he took the time to help her out. Or how sexy she was when she stripped him out of his clothes. When he'd awoken in the darkened room and felt her clamped around his shaft, he relented all the power.

He'd connected with her in a way he didn't know existed. She'd plucked him out of his comfort zone and shoved him into a pair of cowboy boots. He'd spent the day traipsing around outside and the evening getting to know her in the most intimate way. And he'd do it again if given the chance. Frustrated by rejection, he grunted.

"You okay?"

Of course he wasn't okay. But now wasn't the time to get into it, especially in light of how their day had started. "Absolutely. How 'bout some tunes?"

As she raised her phone from her lap, it buzzed. "Damn," she muttered, after staring at the screen.

He glanced over. "What is it?"

"Nothing I can't handle."

"If it's work related, lay it on me. You've got me for one more day. Better make the most of it."

"It's from Tilly, but I don't—"

"Savannah. Read me the text."

"'I'm soooo sorry I gave your mom the hotel info,'" Savannah read. "'She told me she was having some kind of emergency. Now

I'm thinking she was lying. I hope things with your bro are going well. I'm trying to get myself together to meet you in time for the shoot. Not sure it's gonna happen."

The rosy color in Savannah's cheeks had drained and she dropped the phone in her lap. "Unfortunately, this is the end for Tilly and me. What a bummer. She's a great person, but her head isn't in the game any more. I'm going to have to let her go."

"Why?"

"Last night you told me you hadn't been completely honest with me. Well, neither have I, with you." She fiddled with the silver cuff on her ear. "I haven't had an assistant in months. I can manage alone, but a good partner is invaluable. Save for this last minute tourism shoot, Tilly hasn't gotten me a new gig in a while, either. A few months ago, she and her husband opened a coffee shop and, well, you know how that goes. Since then, her priorities shifted."

"How so?" Zander asked.

"For one, she would never have told my mom where I was staying. And, she *should* have discussed my rates with Gerard Ricardo. I was blindsided when he asked about my fees. Tilly agreed to fly in and help me out. Looks like that's not happening."

"I'm sorry." He wanted to pull over, take her in his arms, and comfort her. But he kept on driving. Because that's what an assistant does. He does his job. Period.

"I'm struggling to make ends meet and a friend at the beach offered me a job managing her restaurant," she continued. "Pay is good. Work is steady. I've been holding out, hoping for a sign from the universe to stay on this path. This gig comes along and I think it could be my lucky break. Then, Tilly gets me a meeting with Gerard, but that fizzles."

Zander sorted through what she'd told him. "Since meeting with Gerard, has he told you that you didn't win his business?"

"No, but he might have called Tilly."

"Let's go on the assumption he hasn't decided. What do you

think about sending him a follow-up text letting him know how much you're looking forward to working with him?"

Savannah looked over at him. This time, her smile touched her eyes. "Love it." She unearthed Gerard's business card from her bag and began typing out a message on her phone.

Zander wanted to help because he wanted *her* to be successful. Whatever he could do in the short amount of time they had, he'd do it, ask for nothing, and return home a happier man. Zander had been all about winning. It felt good helping someone else win for a change, even if it meant forgoing his own agenda.

"Here's my first stab at it," she said.

"I'm listening."

"Gerard, it's Savannah Morrissette. Thank you so much for showing me around your club yesterday. I would be thrilled to photograph all three of your properties and know I can capture the beauty of your courses and the elegance of your clubhouses. Have a great vacation."

"That's good. Read it again."

She did.

"What do you think about adding, 'Contact me directly if you have questions.' That keeps the communication between you two. And I'd include a link to your website."

"Great ideas." She added that to the text and eyed Zander one more time. "Okay, I'm sending." Then, she ran her hand down his shoulder and gave his triceps a squeeze. "Thank you."

His arm heated from her touch, but he wasn't going to let his thoughts run wild. Hers was a friendly caress, a sisterly one. While he didn't want that kind of connection with her, it didn't matter. Not this time.

Zander decided to stick with business. This was an area where he was comfortable, proficient even. "Let's circle back to Tilly," he continued. "I have an alternative to firing her, if you're interested."

"Lay it on me."

I'd rather lay myself on you. Shaking away those thoughts, he asked, "What about a compromise? Do you think she might be willing to work part-time while you hunt for a new agent?"

"It doesn't work like that."

"I understand. But if she isn't interested, it's no loss. You were planning on letting her go, anyway."

"It *would* make the conversation easier to have," Savannah said. "I've been avoiding it because we've become such good friends."

"Could you ask her who she recommends you contact for representation? If she's well-networked, she might be willing to help you, especially since you're being so upfront with her."

"She has mentioned other agents to me before." Savannah shot him a smile. "That might work."

"Now, about that assistant…"

He asked a few questions about how she went about finding the right person. They brainstormed her options and she made notes in her phone. When that conversation had been exhausted, he grew quiet.

"You're a smart guy."

"Business is what I do."

"And you do it very well." Her smile was filled with gratitude. Nice, but not nearly enough. He wanted to see desire bursting from her mocha eyes.

"I'm glad to help you out."

They arrived at the Botanical Garden and he searched for a parking spot. After finding one toward the back of the lot, he shifted his attention to her. His heart pounded hard as they stared into each other's eyes. Zander wanted to brush her bangs away from her eyes, capture her face in his hands, and kiss her. But now she really was off-limits. His chest tightened. "Let's get to work."

The morning sun beat down on them, but the cool, dry, morning air whisked away the heat. He breathed deeply, savoring the moment.

He'd never been to a place like this and had no idea what to expect. Why anyone would drive here to check out flowers was beyond him, but the parking lot was almost full.

Like yesterday, she discussed each setup and explained what the art director might want out of a particular picture at a specific location.

"Oh, these blanket flowers are magnificent." She switched lenses and began shooting. When finished, she stepped back. "I love the pop of yellow on the tips of the petals."

To Zander, it was a bunch of wildflowers. "What would you do with that photo?"

"Frame it and give it to someone as a gift or keep it and admire it on my wall. It's not just the beauty of the flower, but a reminder of today. Every day is special. It's the little things that set it apart."

Zander blew through weeks, months even. Head down, focused on his projects, he measured time by the deals he closed or the projects he completed. The past several years had been a blur of activity as he grew his business, but no day stood out as a special one.

He stared at those vibrant flowers like they held the secrets of the universe, but he couldn't shake the emptiness that consumed him. Savannah slid her arm through his and held out the camera, plucking him from his lonely thoughts.

"Smile." She leaned close, held out the camera, and snapped a selfie.

An older gentleman walked over. "You guys want me to take your picture?"

"Sure." Savannah handed him the camera.

"Can you get these flowers in the shot?" Zander asked.

Savannah smiled up at him and he turned toward her while the guy snapped a few pictures. Then, Zander stepped behind her, pulled her flush against him, and wrapped his arms around her. The friendly tourist snapped a few more.

He handed her the camera. "You want to check them out?"

Savannah flipped through the shots on the viewfinder. "They're great. Thanks for stopping."

With a smile, the man wished them a good day and moseyed on.

"Those flowers don't make the day special," Zander said. "You do."

She stilled for a beat, then she lifted her gaze to his. "I'm…so… I like being with you, too."

The atmosphere became charged. He drank her in, trying to memorize every feature, every nuance. It would be effortless to lower his head and kiss her. But he wouldn't disrespect her wishes and cross that line.

"Let's keep going," he suggested.

With a tight nod, she walked ahead. He followed, determined to make the most of their last day together. But those swaying hips and tight ass hijacked his attention. *Dammit. She doesn't want you. Let it go.*

A roadrunner raced past and he pointed it out.

She snapped several shots. "Great sighting."

The sun grew hotter, so he rolled up his sleeves, popped on his shades. Savannah set up test shot after test shot. Her ability to find the right light or the perfect balance of nature continued to astound him. More than once, he found himself mesmerized by the fluid way in which she blended into her surroundings and became one with the environment.

His life revolved around the computer or checking on building structures to ensure they met code. He never stopped long enough to notice a flower or how the breeze cooled his moist skin. Aside from his concern over Kent's health, today was the second day he wasn't plagued with anxiety over finding a new deal or pushing hard for the ones in play to close. Being outside freed his soul and buoyed his spirits. Savannah had given him a gift by sharing her passion with him.

As he shifted his attention to her, he was surprised to see her taking pictures of him. Assuming she needed him in the picture, he basked in the sun's rays.

She approached him and unzipped the bag slung over his shoulder. "You're a beautiful man. The camera loves you."

"I'll keep that in mind in case things don't work out with my company."

"I have a feeling you'll be in business for decades to come."

His stomach dropped. For the first time since he'd started King Development, he wasn't convinced that statement held true. A perfect storm of too many things going wrong at once might sink him and his beloved company.

She finished up at the gardens and they returned to the car. As he rolled back the soft top, she blurted, "No way." Grinning, she spun her phone around to show him. "I heard from Gerard."

Her hand trembled, so he took her phone.

"Savannah," he read out loud. "Thanks for the text. I'm waiting at the airport for my flight and showed my wife your website. She loves your work and thinks you're the right photographer for the job. I've looped my GM into this text. Emily can sign your contract and you two can set up a time to meet. I'll be back in a week. Look forward to working with you."

Savannah's eyes glistened and she swiped away a tear. Then, she cupped Zander's face in her hands. "*You* are a genius." She leaned in. "Zander." Her voice came out in a breathy whisper and her cheeks flushed. "I want…" She swallowed hard, then drifted backward, releasing him. Pulling her sunglasses from the top of her head, she slipped them on, and cleared her throat. "I want to thank you for helping me."

Dammit, woman.

He wanted to haul her into his arms and cover her beautiful face with kisses. Instead, he held out his hand. "Congratulations."

When she slipped hers into his, he ignored the adrenaline surging up his arm. After a single pump, he let go. He hated pulling away. He handed her back her phone and they climbed into the Jeep.

"I was hoping to make a personal detour," she said. "I've always wanted to visit Canyon Road."

He checked his watch along with the destination. "We'll fit it in."

After entering their new stop in his map app, he drove out of the gardens. "What's on Canyon Road?"

"Art galleries."

Ten minutes later, they street parked and sauntered down the sidewalk. Savannah paused in front of a window display to appreciate an artist's work. She turned, her eyes alight with energy. "I love the vibe here. These artists are successful enough to open their own brick and mortar locations. I can't even imagine."

He stepped close, temptingly close. Her sweet scent wafted upward. "Maybe you *should* imagine."

She chuckled. "Yeah, right. The Savannah Morrissette Art Gallery."

They continued on to the next one. 'Scott Brady Art' was emblazoned on the window in gold lettering. "I assisted this photographer right after college."

"Let's go inside," he said.

They walked into the pristine art gallery, the space bright and open. Pictures lined the walls, a small table with chairs hugged the far corner. Other than a group of four chatting in the corner, the store was empty. *How do these artists make a living?*

One of the men glanced over. "Welcome. Let me know if you have questions."

Zander tossed him a nod while staring at the photograph of a flock of geese flying in perfect V formation.

Savannah sidled close, rose on her tiptoes, then laid her hand on his shoulder. Her soft touch sent a heady mix of desire and warmth tumbling through him.

"Check out the price," she whispered in his ear.

He glanced at the tag. "My God, I hope that includes the frame."

He loved her laugh and turned in her direction. She didn't remove her hand from his shoulder and she didn't step away. The air grew electric. Blood whooshed through his veins. He wanted her to back up. If she didn't, he'd kiss her. How in the hell was he supposed to behave appropriately when she stood *this* close?

"Zander, I really—"

"Savannah, is that you?" A man with shoulder-length hair wearing a grungy T-shirt and tattered jeans stood there smiling. "Hey, it *is* you." Before she could detach from Zander, the guy leaned in and gave her a half-hug.

"Scott, hey, it's been a while."

"You look fantastic. Love the hair."

"This is my…" She hesitated. "This is Zander King."

Zander shook his hand. "Good to meet you."

"Are you Savannah's assistant?"

"I'm her managing partner and creative consultant," Zander replied.

Her lips curved at the corners. "I like that."

"I've been following your career," Scott said. "You've done well with landscapes. Where are you living these days?"

She dragged her attention from Zander. "I'm sorry, what?"

"Doesn't matter," he said, shoving his hands into his pockets. "It must be kismet that you strolled in here. I just talked to my agent about you the other day."

"Oh, yeah?" She slowly pulled her arm off Zander's shoulder.

"I'm going on a six-month tour. I could use a good assistant, and I'd be willing to feature some of your pieces. It'll be like old times, only this time we won't have to pool our pennies to split a burger." He gestured around the room. "As you can see, I'm doing okay."

"Congrats on the success. I'm going to pass on the tour,

though." She tucked her hair behind her ear and fiddled with her cuff. "Who's your agent?"

"Heather Costello. She's phenom. You?"

"Tilly Mason, for now."

"If you're shopping for a new one, I can let Heather know." With his hands still tucked into his pockets, he shifted back and forth. "Can I steal you away for a few? Maybe change your mind about the tour?"

Savannah flicked her gaze from one man to the other. "Zander and I are on a tight schedule."

"That's cool." He jogged over to the table and returned with a business card. "Call me and we'll hook up."

I'm sure you'd like that.

She took the card. "Good luck with your tour."

"Good seeing you, doll."

Once they'd walked down the sidewalk, she murmured, "Thirty-five hundred dollars for a shot of geese. He's living in a fantasy-land."

Zander smiled. "One you've been invited into."

She stopped at the next storefront and studied a nude sculpture. "I was his assistant right after college. It was cool back then, but not now."

"What's changed?"

He hadn't expected the intensity pouring from her brown eyes. "Everything."

She was right. Everything *had* changed. And there was no going back to the way things were.

HONESTY

S AVANNAH RAISED HER WINE glass. "To an unforgettable weekend." She clinked Zander's glass and drank, savoring the smooth Chianti before letting the wine slip down her throat.

After hitting the remainder of the Santa Fe locations, they'd headed south toward Albuquerque, stopping for dinner halfway between the two cities at a crowded Mexican restaurant. The sun had set on another special day with her stepbrother. But her heart hurt. She would miss him…a lot.

After sipping the dry, red wine, Zander set his glass on the table. "Today was productive, but we didn't get to the remaining spots in Albuquerque. I'm sorry I can't stay tomorrow, but with Kent's health issue, plus the mountain of problems at work—"

"You've been amazing. Don't even worry about the ones that are left."

"What will you do about those?"

"The shoot starts on Tuesday. I can check them out tomorrow either before or after I meet with Gerard." She smiled. "Sending that text changed everything." She raised her glass again. "You, Zander King, are my hero."

His smile was filled with gratitude. "I just suggested a follow-up. Your talent and professionalism sold him." Being with Zander made her heart beat faster, her insides melt, and her soul soar.

The waitress delivered their entrees and they dug in.

"I want to discuss Starry Cove," she began.

He froze.

"If we're going to overhaul the B&B, it might be a good idea to talk about what else we should do."

Zander set his fork down. "What are you saying, Savannah?"

"I'm having second thoughts about the nature center and a bunch of walking trails that lead to a deserted town."

Initially, she'd dismissed his development project, but now, she wanted to rethink and reassess. He had legitimate motivations for wanting to breathe life into Starry Cove. As much as she loved and appreciated nature, she wasn't convinced that walking trails and a dog park were the best solution to the town's predicament. But neither was the big business of casinos and shopping centers. She'd grown up believing K-Dad's motto: "preserve nature at all costs" wasn't just the right way, it was the *only* way. Now, she wondered if his philosophy had been a tad extreme.

K-Dad's outright rejection of Zander's proposal was flat-out wrong. Since she couldn't ask her stepdad why he'd made that decision, she would do what she believed would best benefit everyone involved.

"Well, that's a big step for you," Zander said.

A little girl popped her head over the booth behind Zander and smiled. Savannah tossed Zander a nod. "You've got a friend."

Zander glanced over his shoulder at the tyke. She grinned at him before flipping back around.

"If we amend your proposed plan, like...say...eliminate the casino or scale things back initially, will the rest of your development still bring in enough tourism to revitalize downtown?" she asked.

He paused for a minute. "I believe it will. The goal is to attract small-town businesses back to Starry Cove while enticing tourism to the new development." He shrugged. "It's okay. I appreciate that you want to help, but I've let that one go."

"Have you given any thought to outside activities like a tour of the town or guided hikes in the nearby mountains? What about rafting? I'm not familiar with the area, but that might be worth checking into. What about offering activities that encourage visitors to put down their phones and appreciate nature for an hour or two?"

"Those are great ideas, Savannah."

The child reappeared with a doll. Zander offered a smile. "Is that your dolly?"

"Yeah, she's new."

Zander's easygoing conversation with the child continued while the family cleared out of the booth.

His thoughtfulness stole Savannah's heart. "Kids like you."

"Guess so." He resumed eating his enchilada.

"I snapped a few pictures of you with that little boy and his parents at our first stop."

"When I was standing in your shot?"

"More like when you were my beautiful muse." She bit into her burrito.

"Your muse?"

And more. "Do you like kids?"

"Love 'em. Kent and Megan have three. I'm at their house a few times a month and spend a lot of time playing with their children."

"Do you want your own?"

"I'd love a family. I'd get involved in my kids' activities, help them with their homework. They say you do the opposite of what your parents did to you. I want to be the kind of dad I wish I'd had. What about you?"

"Gotta find the man before I even considered motherhood. I'd be terrified I'd mess them up."

"Not a chance. You have so much to share. You're smart,

creative, and relaxed. You have a good heart, good intentions. You'd be a great mom."

Savannah reached across the table and blanketed her fingers over his. He regarded their hands before peering into her eyes. She wanted to lean across that table and kiss him, stroke his whiskered face, then apologize for what she'd said earlier. She hadn't meant any of it, but her mom had this way of messing with her head that poisoned everything. Zander hadn't just saved her career, he'd defended her to Debby, which had given her the courage to speak her own mind.

"Thank you for handling Debby and for this entire weekend."

"My pleasure." Every single time they stared into each other's eyes, the energy shifted. "I have every confidence you'll have a great shoot." He pulled his hand away to dig his phone from his pocket. "I should see what flights are available tonight. Might be a red eye."

Stop him. Don't let him leave yet.

He'd been thrown in her life and, two days later, he'd changed it. For a woman who kept things with men low key, traveled the country on a moment's notice, and never had any thoughts of settling down, she'd become quite attached to the man sitting across the table from her.

He'd tossed aside his agenda for hers. He'd put her first and done so much to help her. Not just with the prep for her gig, but in helping her acquire Gerard's business. Initially, she hadn't believed Zander's intentions, but she did now.

What's more, he'd come to her aid when her mother had shown up. No one could get under her skin like Debby. The years of constant manipulation and stealing had taken a toll on Savannah. Before Zander, she'd never talked about it to anyone, not even K-Dad.

She liked this man more than she should and she regretted pushing him away earlier. *What was I thinking? This is a good, good man.*

"Savannah. *Savannah.*"

He plucked her from her thoughts.

"There's a flight at midnight. And another tomorrow morning at six." Intense gray eyes bore into hers. "I'm thinking of taking the one tonight. Are you sure you'll be okay scouting the few remaining locations alone?"

Her chest tightened. She could let him go now or she could steal one more night with him. This amazing man could be hers all night long. She told herself this could never work. They could never be together. They were too different. Her fear of intimacy had ruled her life for as long as she could remember.

For a woman who believed in the power of the universe, she'd done a damn good job of convincing herself to keep a respectable distance from him. Yet, the universe had pushed them together. Why was she fighting what she wanted so desperately?

"Tomorrow."

"I'm sorry, what?"

"I want you to take the flight in the morning."

A low, deep moan shot out of him. "If I stay…"

His words were meant as a warning, but she took them as an invitation. "Yes. Stay. With me."

"Do you know what you're saying?"

Her heart picked up speed. "I didn't mean what I said earlier." She chugged in a deep breath. "I'm sorry. I was pretty rattled after my mom left. You've been incredibly generous with your time, especially with everything going on at your company, and with Kent. I wouldn't have gotten Gerard's gig without your help and I couldn't have prepped this thoroughly without you, either." The tension in her chest loosened. "I don't want you to leave. Stay with me tonight."

He lifted her hand from the table and kissed her finger. "I don't want to leave, either." Then, he turned back to his phone. Another moment later, confidence and determination shone from his beautiful, bright eyes. "Done. Now, let's get the hell out of here."

She couldn't agree more.

Before climbing into the Jeep, she curled her arm around his biceps, and pulled him close. The crisp nighttime air made her shiver and he threw his arms around her and drew her flush against him.

"I can't stop myself," she murmured.

"From what?"

"From you. This shouldn't be happening. It feels too intimate."

"It *is* intimate. It's also real and complicated. We're different in every conceivable way…and we're family." He dipped his head and kissed her. "All I know is that I'm happy when I'm with you. I don't do happy, Savannah. I do miserable, tortured, and obsessed." He kissed her again. "Those don't exist when we're together."

He kissed her yet again, this time dipping his tongue inside her mouth. Groaning, she buried her fingers in his hair. This man was making her quake in the best way possible.

He slowed the kiss, finishing with tender pecks on her lips. "That should hold us."

"What am I going to do with you?" she murmured.

Even in the darkness, his eyes shone with mischief. "You're the creative one. I'm sure you'll think of something." He opened the passenger door and she climbed inside.

He leaned in and kissed her once more before walking around and sliding behind the wheel. Then, in the darkened vehicle, he murmured, "I don't want to hold back with you."

"My God, you are so honest."

"I'll always be honest with you." He started the engine and headed out of the parking lot. "How can wrong feel this damn right?"

"Maybe it's not wrong."

When he placed his hand on her thigh, she interlocked her fingers with his. A few miles passed before she fiddled with her playlist. "Do you like KT Tunstall?"

"I'm not familiar with that artist."

After Savannah pulled up "Black Horse and the Cherry Tree", she pulled his hand back onto her lap, caressed his fingers, and gazed into the night sky. Their weekend had been special. Friday felt like a lifetime ago. *Hard to believe so much has happened.*

Zander had stirred her heart in ways she'd never thought possible. How could someone so committed to big business be the one person she loved being with? His transformation had been thrilling to witness. The constant knot between his brows had cleared. He smiled more. He had stepped out of his comfort zone with a steadiness she admired. When he'd allowed her to switch up his duds, the clothing had changed him. Or maybe her opinion of him had changed when she'd dressed him in something else. Looking back, she wasn't sure which had happened first.

When he was by her side, anything was possible. Anything at all.

"What's going on in that beautiful head of yours?"

"Thinking about all the things you've done for me in the past few days and how you've changed my life for the better."

He squeezed her hand before letting go. "I've loved every minute of our weekend. You're a special woman, Savannah."

His words made her heart beat faster.

Savannah guarded her feelings, but Zander made her feel safe. She could be herself without fear that he would manipulate her or shame her or lie to her. This was a good man who had gone the extra mile because she needed a helping hand.

He pulled into a shopping center and parked near the grocery store. "I'm running in to grab condoms. If I've misread you, now would be the time to stop me."

Leaning over, she planted a kiss on him. "Get a dozen," she said and winked.

When Zander returned to the Jeep, Savannah was on the phone.

"Glad you got the coffee shop back in order," she said. "I want to update you on a couple of things if you have a minute."

She set her hand on his thigh and caressed his leg. He started to harden. There was no turning back now. Even if he wanted, he couldn't keep himself in check. He liked his stepsister…a lot.

"Zander has been a big help. I've got a few more spots to scout and I'll knock those out tomorrow. I'd still love your assist on the shoot, but no worries if you can't get here."

More listening.

"Sure. Let me know." She paused. "I heard from Gerard. I got the golf club gig."

Zander could hear Tilly's shouts as he started the Jeep. Savannah leaned over and kissed his cheek.

"Landing that job is huge and I'm ready to take my career to the next level." Savannah inhaled and blew out the breath in a whoosh. "This is difficult for me, but I'm thinking we should work together part-time until I find a new agent. What do you think?"

Zander drove out of the lot and merged into traffic, heading toward the hotel.

After a long silence, Savannah said, "I feel the same." Another pregnant pause. "If you have any recommendations of who I should contact, let me know."

Tilly spoke for another moment before the call ended.

"Whew, I'm glad that's over." Savannah tucked her phone into her handbag.

"What did she say?" Zander asked.

"She's going to contact a few of her agent friends she thinks would be a good fit for me."

"I think she'll come through for you."

"I would never have said anything to her if we hadn't talked about it. So, thank you." She peeked in the bag. "Just a three-pack?"

He chuckled. "Aren't you the feisty one?"

"You're too much fun not to take full advantage of."

"You're the fun one, Savannah. I'm just along for the ride."

They returned to the hotel and hurried into their room. Before the door had banged shut, she jumped into his arms and kissed him full-out. A clash of lips and teeth and tongues sent a burst of adrenaline careening through him.

He couldn't hold her close enough or kiss her hard enough. The intensity with which she clung to him left him gasping for air. "My God, woman, you are insatiable."

"You're leaving me and I need to get my fill of you."

Gasping for breath, he cradled her face in his hands. "I'm not leaving you, Savannah. My work here is done. You don't need me anymore."

Despite her silence, the sadness in her eyes told him otherwise. Her rueful smile tore at his heart.

One layer at a time, he disrobed her until she stood naked before him. He drank her in, her beautiful form stealing his breath and his mind. Savannah's soft, feminine shoulders and full breasts gave way to an hourglass waist and full hips. He loved a woman with a round backside and, as he pulled her close and ran his hand over her derrière, he moaned. Her bottom was perfect. "You're a striking woman."

She tilted her face toward his, a smile dancing on the corners of her luscious mouth. He kissed her before toeing out of his boots. Then, he waited while she peeled off his clothing, stepped flush against him and trailed her hands down his back until they came to rest on his ass.

She scraped her fingernails up his back and over his shoulders, then cat-scratched his whiskered cheeks. Her gaze never left his. Her breathing had fallen in line with his, too.

He captured her hand in his and kissed each finger, the fire in her eyes igniting his own blaze. Excitement pulsed through him and, as she sprang up on her tiptoes, he snaked his arm around her waist.

"I want to make the most of our time together." Again, his mouth found hers while her soft moans sent streaks of desire pounding a hard line to his shaft.

She trembled in his arms.

"Are you cold?" he asked while stroking her back.

"No, I'm scared."

With gentle fingers, he brushed her hair off her brow. "Of what?"

"Real intimacy," she said and hugged him.

Her revealing words touched his heart. He tightened his hold, dropped a tender kiss on her bare shoulder. Wrong didn't just feel right. It felt necessary. An absolute. Like he couldn't let her go because he'd be empty and soulless without her.

"That's exactly what this is," he said staring into her eyes. "And it feels—you feel—right."

When he traced her cheek with the backs of his fingers, she slipped her hand between their bodies and wrapped delicate fingers around his erection. Then, she anchored her other hand on his shoulder and rose up to kiss him.

The sensation of her touch skyrocketed his need. She responded to his grunts and groans with gritty moans. He sunk his hands into the hair framing either side of her face and kissed her breathless. Panting, she broke away, her lids heavy with desire.

"Inside me," she gasped. "Please."

They tumbled into bed.

He kissed her, letting his tongue swirl slowly with hers. Her sexy moans blended with his. He fondled her breast, brushing his thumb across her swollen nipple. She caressed his back and clawed his shoulders, but when she fisted his hair and tugged, he knew she couldn't wait another second.

"Sit against the pillows," she rasped out.

Eager to comply, he moved into position and sheathed himself. She straddled him and, after positioning him at her opening, she sunk down. Her throaty moan filled his ears while he groaned through the pleasure.

"I need this." She cupped his face in her hands and kissed him. "I need *you.*"

But she didn't start moving. Instead, she kissed one cheek, then the other. Then, she rested her forehead on his so they could share each other's breath. Being inside her, being as connected as two people can be, revitalized his body and soothed his soul. This woman...*this* woman. *I cannot get enough of her.*

Slowly, she started gliding, the waves of pleasure numbing his mind. When she rose up and positioned her breast near his mouth, he tasted one erect nipple and then the other. The harder he sucked and nibbled, the faster she glided. Their sexy pants, moans, and cries undid him, urging toward an explosive release.

"You feel incredible," she murmured.

"So do you," he whispered, while jolts of pleasure radiated through him. He captured her face in his hands and kissed her. No matter how deeply he was nestled inside her, he wanted to be closer.

Her moans turned guttural and she threw her head back, closed her eyes. He massaged her breasts as she increased her speed. His cock throbbed, the orgasm threatening to burst out of him.

"Savannah, I'm close. Slow down, if you want me to wait."

Curling her fingers over his shoulders, she pinned him with a searing gaze. "Let go and let me take you."

He gripped her hips to guide her, and the intensity of their lovemaking turned primal. She took him faster and deeper, daggering her nails into his skin and moaning.

He surrendered to her, the euphoria surging through him.

Panting, he captured her face in his hands, pulled her toward him, and kissed her hard.

"For you," he said. "I want all this to be for you. Let me touch you."

"Don't stop," she gasped.

Continuing to glide on his erection, she rubbed her clit while he pinched her nipple and stroked her ass.

As she gazed into his eyes, her insides tightened around him. "I'm so turned on by you. I…I…oh, oh, Zander."

"You're so sexy. Let go, Savannah."

Her wild, raspy groans intensified, and she glided with a frenzied urgency. She was unraveling around him. When he anchored his hand around her neck and pulled her close, she shuddered and cried out, trembling in his arms as she shattered around him.

Then, she kissed him with such intensity he was convinced he could never let her go. He kissed her again and again until she collapsed against him. He wrapped his arms around her and hugged her.

Sated, they lay together, arms and legs entwined. Savoring her in his arms, he caressed her soft skin. Moments passed with nothing but the sound of their gentle breathing and tender touching. Tranquility settled over him.

"Mmm," she murmured, when he dropped a worshipful kiss on her forehead.

"Good for you?"

She peeked up at him. "You're addictive. You?"

"Same here."

She kissed his chest and dragged her tongue over his nipple. "Where's that necktie you wore at the reading of the will?"

"Packed."

"I can think of a much better use for that clothing accessory. Let's get it out."

"My wild, wild stepsister." He kissed her.

The corners of her lips quirked. "It's you, brother. It's all you."

His cock twitched. "Again?"

"You read my mind."

His muscles grew taught. "This time, my way."

"And what is your way?" she asked, caressing the curve of his biceps.

"Dirty," he replied. "Very, *very* dirty."

14

WHATEVER IT TAKES

FOUR O'CLOCK IN THE morning came way too quickly. Savannah slunk out of bed, switched on the desk lamp, and started dressing.

Zander leaned up on his elbows. "What are you doing?"

She found his sleepy face adorable. "I'm taking you to the airport." She reached around and hooked her bra into place.

"Savannah." He pushed out of bed and stroked her shoulders, sending tingles across her skin. "You don't have to. I can call for a ride."

"I want to. Plus, I'm going to photograph the sunrise."

"It'll give us a few more minutes together."

She couldn't miss the sadness in his voice.

He dressed in his suit, no tie. Though the etched lines between his eyebrows were gone, the tailored clothes were a sobering reminder that Zander King was a businessman first and foremost.

He stared at himself in the mirror. "What the hell am I doing?"

"Getting ready to fly home."

"Not in this, I'm not." He changed into jeans and his new black shirt.

"Much better." Sidling up behind him, she curled her arms

around his muscular abdomen and hugged him. "An uptight suit flew west, but a rugged outdoorsman heads east. The ladies are going to *love* the new you."

She let him go and he turned to face her. "There's only one woman I want to impress."

"And who would that be?"

"My stepsister. Actually, she's my former stepsister and the only family I've got. Gotta hang on to that woman."

"Guess you want to keep in touch?"

Laughing, he slid into his black dress shoes. "Good assumption."

When he finished getting ready, he shouldered his bag and opened the door. She breezed through, this time slowing to kiss him. "I'll miss you," she whispered before continuing into the hallway.

"You're going to be too busy working to give me a second thought. I'll be the one doing all the missing."

On the short drive to the airport, she had to touch him, had to feel the warmth of his skin pressing hers, so she clasped his hand.

Though she tried being rational about their situation, her heart was breaking. Regardless of how or why they'd reconnected, she cared about this man. More than she dared to admit.

Zander's phone buzzed. "Kent's calling. I've got to take this." He punched the talk key and hit the speaker button. "Hey, how are you doing?"

"I've been better."

Zander shifted in his seat. "Did you have a setback?"

"Physically, I'm good, all things considered. I got your text that you're flying back today. Are you at the airport?"

"No, Savannah's driving me there now. You're on speaker. You remember Savannah, don't you?"

"Hey, Savannah, it's been a while."

"Hi, Kent. How are you feeling?"

"Doing okay. You guys get a lot accomplished?"

"Much more than anticipated," Zander replied, throwing Savannah a smile. "What's going on?"

As Savannah followed the airport signs, her throat constricted, the emotion threatening to spill out of her.

"Call me after you check in," Kent said. "It's about Esteem University."

Zander took Kent off speaker. "Can you fill me in now?" As he listened, he rubbed his forehead. "*Arrested?* I can't believe this. I just spoke with the president yesterday."

Savannah could hear Kent, but she couldn't make out what he was saying.

"This is the worst news," Zander said. "They screwed their students, their investors and they *totally* screwed us." While listening, he cracked the window. "Where does that leave us?"

She could feel the tension rolling off him as he continued listening. His brow glistened with a light sheen of perspiration.

"We'll have to file for bankruptcy and regroup." Zander couldn't hide the disappointment in his voice.

Oh, no. What happened? Savannah's stomach dropped as she pulled up to the curb for departures. Despite the early hour, the airport bustled with activity.

Zander flung open the door, but remained rooted in the seat. "Let's keep this between us until we can figure out what to tell the team. I'll swing by as soon as I land."

After hanging up, he pushed out. Savannah waited on the sidewalk while he collected his overnight bag from the back.

"That call didn't sound good," she said.

She didn't buy his forced smile. "Just a work issue. Will you be okay scouting those remaining locations on your own today?"

"Zander, I'll be fine. Please tell me."

"This has been a wonderful—no, a *perfect* weekend." He drew her into his arms and hugged her. "Text me and let me know how the shoot goes."

Their kiss was tender, filled with a gentleness that lingered on her lips. Her feelings for this man were a dangerous elixir that conjured up more emotions than she knew how to process.

He whispered a goodbye and, then, he was gone. Her heart broke as he walked inside and vanished in a sea of travelers. She shuddered in a breath, tears filling her eyes. She had always believed K-Dad was the best man she'd ever known.

But now she knew the truth. His son was.

———

POWERING TOWARD THE TICKET counter, Zander wiped the sweat from his brow. How could such an extraordinary weekend have ended this miserably? *The universe wants to keep things in check, A-hole. One minute, I've got a company and no woman. The next, I've got no company and I'm staring into the eyes of an amazing woman. Maybe that'll teach me not to screw my stepsister.*

According to Kent, their Esteem project was dead. The president and CFO had been lying to everyone about the organization's finances, and several hundred million dollars was missing and unaccounted for. They'd cooked their books to show a profit, but they were running in the red. Instead of having a hundred thousand students, the online university had a mere forty-five hundred. They'd defrauded their investors and business partners, King Development being one of them. The government had frozen their assets and key executives had been arrested. *We're finished.*

With no other opportunities of this magnitude on the docket, they couldn't bounce back. And in light of Kent's health issue, he doubted his business partner would be in a position to start up another venture. Nausea clouded his thoughts. He closed his eyes hoping to stave off the whopper of a headache barreling toward him.

The check-in line snaked back and forth so many times he

questioned whether he'd get to his gate in time. *Figures. I won't make my flight. But I'd get to spend the day with Savannah.*

The line plodded along. His fingers twitched to call Kent back and ask him to repeat himself. But he didn't need confirmation. He needed to wake from this hellish nightmare. His phone buzzed. Despite wanting to ignore it, he pulled it from his pocket.

"Where are you?" texted Savannah. "I'm in the airport."

When he didn't see her, he texted back, "Standing in the long line that's weaving…"

Someone touched his arm and he pivoted. As soon as Savannah threaded her arms around his waist, calmness blanketed him.

"Hey," she murmured.

"What are you doing here? What happened to capturing that sunrise?"

"I've got dozens of sunrise shots and only one chance to help you." Big brown eyes blinked up at him. "I can't let you leave knowing something is wrong. You've gotta talk to me."

"Savannah, you have enough on your—"

Hands on hips, she pursed her lips. "Spill it, King."

"We lost a hundred and twenty-five million on a project that ended abruptly when the executives got arrested for fraud."

Her eyes grew large. "Oh, wow, that's bad. So, you're out the money?"

"Looks that way."

"Don't you have other projects?"

"We do, but those can't generate the cash needed to pay back the loan we'd taken."

"Does this mean the company is bankrupt?"

"It's worse. We won't be able to bounce back from this. We'll have to shut down." He pressed his temple to soothe the throbbing.

The line inched ahead and they shuffled forward.

She broke eye contact for several seconds. "Would the Starry Cove project save your company?"

"Savannah, you don't—"

She crossed her arms. "Answer my question, Zander."

"Yes, it would."

"Am I the only thing standing in the way of making this happen?"

He nodded. "Yes."

"Just because we didn't resolve the Starry Cove issue doesn't mean I haven't been thinking about it. I'd planned on contacting Sheldon and surprising you." She smiled up at him. "I've changed my mind. You have my full support."

He stared at her for several seconds, questioning whether he'd heard her correctly.

She squeezed his shoulders. "Starry Cove. Remember that one?"

With his heart beating out of his chest, he enveloped her in his arms and dropped a kiss on her forehead. "Are you sure? You were dead set against it."

"I don't want The Town that Time Forgot to become a tacky tourist trap. But I believe we can revive the area while maintaining its natural beauty. Initially, I wanted to follow K-Dad's wishes without considering how that decision would affect the bigger picture. I made assumptions about you and I was wrong."

Staring in disbelief at his stepsister, Zander fought against the welling emotion. "Thank you. So much."

She brushed hair from her eyes. "I can do for you what K-Dad could not. As much as I adored that man, I'm not making the same mistake he did."

"What mistake was that?"

"Rejecting you outright because, at first pass, I disagree. You opened my eyes, too. You're a good man, you're open to change, and you put me before you." Her gaze flitted over his face. "I believe you'll do right by that town and you'll do right by me, too. The magic lives in discovering that middle ground and I have every confidence we'll find it."

Tears pricked his eyes. He dipped his head, brushed his lips against hers. "You didn't just save King Development, you saved me."

"Right back atcha." She hugged him. "Let's draft an email to Sheldon. He can have the paperwork ready by the time you land. We'll make this project work so we both win."

So we both win. For a man who'd spent his life pushing to be number one, he liked the sound of that...a lot.

15

THE BEST SURPRISE

W HEN ZANDER'S FLIGHT LANDED at Dulles, he exited the plane, found a quiet spot at a deserted gate, and read the email from Sheldon.

Savannah and Zander,

Per your email, and my detailed conversation with Savannah, you're moving forward with the renovation of Starry Cove. Outlined below are your terms of agreement.

In addition to the walking trails and dog park, the one hundred acres of undeveloped land will be renovated according to the King Development proposal, with the following changes:

(1) the casino is excluded, (2) the shopping outlet is in flux, but both parties have agreed to continue discussions and come to a compromise, and (3) outdoor activities will be offered that promote physical activity with a focus on nature.

The emotion that Zander fought to control earlier threatened to escape again. He stared out the window, reflecting back on how the weekend had played out. If he hadn't stepped outside his comfort zone and jumped on that plane, he would be facing a very different scenario. But the real win wasn't the business deal. It was Savannah.

In short order, she'd captured his heart without even trying. Her carefree spirit and love of nature had breathed life into his stuffy, lost soul. Despite being in a constant state of frustration, he was living to work and pushing to win. And he was miserable. She didn't just make him happy; she made him want to be a better person.

He replied to Sheldon and Savannah, agreeing to the terms, and sent the email. Then, he texted her. "I miss you."

Dots appeared. "Good."

He smiled. "How's the scouting going?"

"Great. The art director is thrilled I checked out so many locations. Couldn't have done it without you."

"Pleasure was all mine. I'll call you later."

"Sure you will, Slick."

With a grin, he closed that text thread and opened the one with Kent.

"On my way," he texted.

"I'm here," Kent replied.

Forty-five minutes later, Zander parked in front of Kent's home, nestled in a northern Virginia neighborhood where bikes were strewn on front yards and a slew of kids played basketball in the court. The Walker home was filled with children and chaos... and love.

As he rang the doorbell, he smiled. He couldn't wait to tell Kent the good news.

Megan Walker swung open the door, concern etched on her pretty face. She wore a long sleeved T-shirt and leggings, her hair tied in a loose ponytail. "I'm glad you're here. It's been a stressful few days."

Zander stepped into their two-story foyer and gave her a hug. "How are you holding up?"

"Better now that Kent's back home." She eyed his facial hair.

"Nice scruff. I heard you took a mini-vacation. Or did Kent tell me that so I'd stop worrying?"

"I flew to New Mexico for the weekend. I wish I could have stayed longer. When Kent gets the go ahead from his doc, you guys should fly out there. It's a beautiful state. Awesome mountain views. Great food. Friendly people."

Her eyebrows shot up. "Were you abducted by aliens and dropped off in Roswell? You've never once taken time off from work. Maybe there's hope for you two yet." She crossed her arms over her chest. "Hey... you're not wearing a suit."

Kent's three-year-old came toddling around the corner wearing nothing but a Pull-Up. "Unky Zader!"

Grinning, Zander picked him up. "There's my little buddy. Phew, you stink."

"I poopy in my big boy pants," Colin said.

Zander handed him over to Megan. "Potty training?"

"I...I do pee-pee in da toilet."

Zander smiled at the child. "That's great, Colin."

"Stay and pay with me. I got a new truck from my Gammy and Poppy."

"Absolutely. I'm going to talk to your daddy first."

"Okay." He held up three pudgy fingers. "Tree minutes. And don't be late, 'kay?"

Megan laughed. "Kent's mini-me." With Colin perched on her hip, she started up the stairs. "He's in the family room. We'll be back."

Kent lay sprawled on the sofa watching TV, while the baby shook a rattle in his exersaucer. His partner did a double take. "What the—you've got facial hair. Are those jeans?"

After bending down to hug his friend, Zander sat on the floor beside the youngest Walker.

He grinned at the tot. "Hi, little one."

The baby's toothless smile and garbled chatter made Zander chuckle.

"What's with the clothes?" Kent asked. "You look good, bro."

"I had a wardrobe makeover, amongst other things. How are you? You scared the hell out of me."

"Megan's in charge now." Smiling, Kent rolled his eyes. "I ate a raw kale salad last night. And we're going to start walking together."

"She loves you and wants you healthy. You better listen to her."

"We're going to have to put together a press release." Kent picked up the tablet on the coffee table in front of him. "I've drafted something I can read you."

Zander spun one of the toys on the saucer and the baby giggled. "I've got news."

"Oh, God." Kent swung his legs off the sofa and sat up. "I don't know how much more I can handle."

"We got the Starry Cove deal."

While Kent gaped at Zander, the baby pounded on the exersaucer. Zander held out his hand and the little one gripped his finger.

"Say that again," Kent said.

"The Starry Cove project is a 'go.'"

"Are you for real? You're messing with me, aren't you?"

"It's the truth. I was as surprised as you are, but it's happening."

"How'd you pull that off?"

"When my dad passed, he left the land parcel to us, expecting Savannah to carry out his wishes. Initially, she didn't want to change a thing." Zander smiled. "I'll spare you the long story, but suffice it to say, she's on board. Details will be ironed out in the coming weeks."

"And the devil lives in those details. Talk to me."

"She wants us to partner with green companies."

"We already do that."

"See how easy this is going to be?"

Kent laughed.

"No buildings can impede the mountain views, the sunrises or the sunsets. She wants structures to complement the natural surroundings. Stucco—or Parex—over cement, for example."

"Sounds more than reasonable."

The baby pulled Zander's finger into his mouth, so Zander handed him his teething ring. "And no casino."

"I can live with that. What about the shopping outlet?"

"Unresolved for the moment, but discussions are underway. Also, Savannah would like us to explore incorporating physical activity into the offering. Like tours of the historic town, guided hikes in the mountains, that kind of thing. She loves nature and wants to share her passion. You know, something like 'Stop living in a virtual world and start playing in the real one.'"

A smile spread over Kent's face. "That's fantastic. I love it."

"Like I said, her requirements are reasonable."

"Holy Hell. She saved us." Pushing off the sofa, Kent extended his hand to Zander.

Zander rose and shook it. "Yeah, big time."

"This is huge." Grinning like a happy fool, Kent pulled Zander in for a backslapping man hug.

Megan breezed into the room, Colin locked on her hip. "And now you two are *hugging*? I can't keep up with all these changes." With a playful smile, she plunked her son down on the carpet and he wheeled over a large fire truck.

"Pay with me, Unky."

Zander sat on the floor and rolled the truck around while making a siren noise.

"Honey," Kent said. "The Starry Cove deal is on."

Megan flicked her gaze between the two men. "Oh, my! Does that mean what I think it means?"

"We're staying afloat," Zander replied.

Megan's eyes filled with tears and she threw her arms around her husband. "I'm super relieved. I've been scared sick you'd have to look for a job. That's too stressful right now."

Kent kissed her. "It's all good, honey."

"But we've got to retool," Zander continued. "Slow things down, take the company in a different direction."

"Who *is* this man?" Megan asked her husband.

Kent kissed the baby and ruffled Colin's head of blond hair before returning to the sofa. "A laid-back version of himself, that's for sure. Maybe he'd like to stay for dinner."

"Stay, Unky, stay!" Colin squealed.

"I'd love to." If Zander went home to an empty condo, he'd spend the evening thinking about Savannah. He'd done plenty of that on the flight home.

"We're having baked chicken, salad, and quinoa," Megan said.

"Sounds great." Kneeling, Zander rolled the truck over to Colin who'd started building with his Lego Duplo blocks.

Megan pulled the baby from the exersaucer, kissed his chubby cheek, and sat on the floor with him between her legs. "Zander, you look…well, you look great. Can I assume a woman is responsible for this change?"

He smiled. "I reconnected with someone from my past."

"Oh, wow," Kent blurted.

"What?" Megan asked. "Do you know her?"

"I did, years ago," Kent replied.

"She's my former stepsister," Zander said. "My dad married her mom when we were kids. Our folks stayed together for something like eight years. Due to the terms of my dad's will, Savannah and I were forced to work together. Turns out, we're complete opposites, yet totally compatible."

"She must be perfect for you because *you*, Zander King, are a different man." Megan handed the baby a rattle. "I'm happy for you and I can't wait to meet her."

"Aside from you two, I have no intention of discussing our family history with anyone."

"Understandable," Kent said. "You've been apart for how long?"

Pausing, Zander did the math. "Seventeen years. I was eighteen the last time I saw her."

"Ancient history," Kent said. "You two aren't blood related. Plus, your blended past is nobody's business."

"I agree," Megan said. "About five years ago, two of my relatives, who are second cousins, eloped. At first, there was a big brouhaha. Now, no one cares." She turned the baby around, made a silly face, and he started giggling. "What does *she* think?"

"Good question," Zander replied. "I'll have to ask her."

Kent's five-year-old daughter, Katrina, entered the room and beamed at Zander. "Hi, Uncle Zander." She plopped down on the floor next to him, her small hand clutching a Barbie. She showed him her doll. "What should her job be? She's been a nurse. My other Barbie is a teacher. My *other* other Barbie is a football player. This one is my favorite." The child held out the doll for Zander to see.

After a moment, he said, "What about a photographer?"

"A what?" Katrina asked.

"A person who takes pictures."

"What could she take pictures of?"

"Lots of things," Zander said. "Sunsets or mountains or animals or even pictures of people."

"Okay, that's good." The child scrambled to her feet and bounded out of the room.

"A photographer," Megan said. "Well, that answers that question."

Zander couldn't help but smile. Savannah was tattooed on his brain. His phone chirped with an incoming photo from her. He unlocked his phone and tapped on the picture. It was one the guy had snapped of them together.

"From Savannah?" Megan asked.

Zander spun the phone around.

"She's beautiful. You two look great together."

"She's pretty amazing." Just thinking about her made him so damned happy.

"Congratulations on Starry Cove *and* on your new relationship," Megan said. "I'll pour us drinks. We'll celebrate."

Kent shook his head. "And by drinks she means Pomegranate juice and sparkling water."

"Heart healthy, honey." With the baby in her arms, Megan kissed her husband. "Zander, we're going to eat a little early so Kent and I can take a stroll after dinner."

"I'll stay with the kids if you want," Zander said.

"Wow," Megan said. "Just wow."

"You know I love your children," Zander replied.

"I do, but you've never offered to watch them. I like the new you," she said, as she scooted toward the kitchen.

"Need help, Meg?" Kent asked.

"I'm good," she called over her shoulder.

Zander stared at the photo. He looked happy and relaxed. And the only way to stay that way would be to keep Savannah in his life. "You're too gorgeous for a guy like me," he texted back.

"My beautiful stepbrother." She added a winking face emoji. "We look good together."

Megan returned with the non-alcoholic mixture in wine glasses and a sippy cup for Colin. "I'm running to the grocery store and I'll bring the baby with me. Can you keep an eye on Colin and Katrina?"

"Tell Kat to play down here, so I'm not running up and down the stairs to check on her," Kent said.

"Okay. Be back in twenty." She kissed Colin and Kent before leaving the room.

Kent clicked off the TV and raised a goblet. "To Savannah, for saving our butts."

The two men clinked glasses and drank down the sparkling beverage.

"Alright, let's see the photo," Kent said.

Zander handed him his phone.

"That's Vanna? She's beautiful."

"She goes by Savannah now, and yeah, she is. Look at me. I'm wearing jeans, and I can't stop smiling."

Both men laughed.

"So, what's happening with you two?"

"I don't know where to start." Zander offered Colin a Lego block. "You need this one, buddy."

The youngster snatched the long, blue piece.

"Colin, what do you say to Uncle Zander?" Kent asked.

"Tanks."

"Good job," Kent said. "Hey, Zander, it's me you're talking to."

Zander added blocks to Colin's tower. "You know I'm a rule follower."

"Always have been. What does that have to do with Savannah?"

"Having a—" he glanced at Colin—"an *interpersonal* relationship with a family member felt taboo."

"But you're *not* related."

"No, we're not. But she was my stepsister for eight years and the only family I have."

"How'd you work through it?"

"Short answer? I couldn't imagine my life without her." Zander handed Colin another block.

"Tank you."

Zander patted the tyke's back. "Sure thing, buddy."

"Good job, Colin," Kent said.

"Having her in my life outweighs what other people might think." Zander shot his friend a smile. "Plus, my gut tells me she's the one."

"Then she must be," Kent said. "Because your gut is rarely wrong."

TRUE PARTNERS

TWO WEEKS LATER, ZANDER strode into Dulles Airport, slowing to scan the arrivals board. Savannah's flight had just landed and he couldn't wait to see her.

While waiting at the security gate, his hands grew clammy. He didn't get rattled easily, but today, he was putting it all out there. He was stepping out of his comfort zone by taking a risk in the romance department. *Gotta man up.*

Zander knew his way around a construction site. He was comfortable in a boardroom. Corporate meetings were a breeze. He could manage through most situations, save one.

Navigating matters of the heart were foreign to him. He didn't know the first thing about the language of love. But he *did* know that he had fallen in love with Savannah, and he had to figure out a way to blend their individual lives so they could have a shot at something real and long-lasting.

Love meant being vulnerable. Love meant fifty-fifty. Love also could mean loss, abandonment, and heartache. Zander didn't want to get it wrong like his father had, over and over again.

If he could build a small empire from nothing, he could muster up a few heartfelt words and the guts to speak them.

People hurried by, but no Savannah. Then, he spotted her, and his heart pounded out of his chest. She wore a fitted white shirt, black dress pants, and heels. *Professional and gorgeous.* He couldn't take his eyes off her. Seeing her reconfirmed his feelings. *I love her.*

She glanced in his direction, then did a double take. A huge smile spread over her face as she hurried over to him. "I thought we were meeting in Starry Cove." She set down her camera bags and hugged him. "What are you doing here?"

"Surprising you." He pulled her close, fearing that if he let go, she would slip away. For someone who steered clear of commitment, holding her felt right...and freeing. "Welcome home." He kissed her, relishing her soft lips pressed to his. "Let's grab your bag and get out of here."

While walking to baggage claim, she inspected him. "That's a great look."

He'd worn black jeans, a brown quarter-zip sweater, and a black sport coat, along with black dress boots.

"Glad you like. I dressed for you." He squeezed her hand. "You look gorgeous."

Locking gazes with him, she smiled. "Don't we have an investor's meeting today?"

"They rescheduled for tomorrow, pending your availability."

"That'll work."

Having her by his side felt phenomenal. Video chatting and texting hadn't been enough. He needed her in his life every single day. Blood whooshed through his veins and he shuddered in a breath. He wasn't cut out for all this interpersonal stuff, but he had to tell her how he was feeling.

While luggage tumbled onto the carousel, he asked about her conversation with Heather, a prospective new agent.

"I was all ready to sign with her until Scott Brady, the guy—"

"I remember him. The artist who invited you to sleep...er, I mean, *tour* with him."

She laughed. "You're not jealous, are you?"

"Jealous? No. Suspicious? Hell yeah." He threaded his fingers through hers and caressed her skin with his thumb. Even their tender connection ratcheted up the heat.

"I'm not interested in him." She leaned up, kissed his scruffy cheek. "He called me to tell me how stoked Heather was after we spoke."

"I'm glad it worked out for you."

"It did, but not in the way you think. She pretty much shared our entire conversation with him and he repeated it all back to me when he called me."

Zander shook his head. "That's unprofessional."

"Sure was. I declined her offer for representation. But, Tilly came through for me. I'm glad I listened to you and didn't just fire her. She introduced me to an agent friend who's a great fit and I signed with her yesterday."

"Congratulations. I've got your back, babe."

"*Babe*. Mmm, I like that," she said while caressing his back. Desire and comfort coursed through him.

Zander grabbed her bag and they walked out of the airport. "You okay leaving your vehicle here?"

"I'll grab my truck on the way back. I can afford six bucks a day." She smiled. "Shooting Gerard's courses made all the difference."

"I hope that job lands you twenty more." After ushering her into his Range Rover, he snagged one more kiss before setting off toward Starry Cove.

"What did Gerard say when you showed him the shots?"

"He loved them. His wife did, too. She had a better eye for what would work, so she selected most of the photos. He's already recommended me to two of his friends who own golf clubs in Arizona and California."

"Nice."

"If they hire me, I'm hoping I can steal you away for a few days." She caressed his thigh.

His body heated from her repetitive touch. "I'd be happy to help you."

"No help needed. I want to take you on a getaway…and play."

He flashed her a grin. "I'll play with you."

"I can't wait," she said. "I'm dying for you, baby."

"Me, too. But we've got some business to take care of first."

"Making me wait for the good stuff, huh?"

He drew her hand to his lips and kissed her soft skin. "I promise it'll be worth it."

"You sound pretty confident in your lovemaking abilities, Mr. King. Are you *sure* you want to make such a bold claim?"

He chuffed out a laugh. "All the credit goes to you. You bring out the best in me."

"You charmer you, but I think you have something to do with it."

He jumped on the Dulles Greenway, heading west. "Did you see Sheldon's email about Kyle's remains?"

"Yeah. I like your idea about scattering his ashes in Starry Cove."

"We'll do it together." He held her gaze an extra second before turning back to the road. *I'm about to propose we do a lot of things together.*

"How's Kent doing?"

"He's cut back from sixty hours a week to forty, and he's taking better care of himself. He and Megan want to have us over for dinner this weekend."

"Sounds great. What did you tell them about us?"

"*Us*. I like that."

Smiling, she shifted in her seat. "Well, we co-own a hundred acres of land, a B&B, oh, and a huge Victorian home. You've video chatted me almost every day, you text me all the damn time, and you've shared your bad-boy fantasies with me, one of which I was happy to assist you with from afar."

He grinned at her. "I did share those with you, didn't I?"

"Yes, you did, and they were *spicy*." She caressed his whiskered cheek with the back of her fingers. "Did your friends comment on our unconventional relationship?"

"Kent is thrilled for us. Megan couldn't get over the change in me. She can't wait to meet you." He glanced over. "They both agreed with me that our family history is our business. I want you to know if word got out, I would address it. I'm not easily intimidated. You mean more to me than any backlash that might come our way."

"As an artist, I've been subjected to reviews of my work for years. Some criticize my photographs, while others love them. I learned early on, I can't let their opinions rule my emotions or my life. *You* make me happy. And my happiness is more important than the opinions and biases of others."

"Well said."

"In the short time we've been together, we've had each other's back. If someone said something hurtful or out of line, I think we'd handle it *together* and move on."

"I know we would." He laid a possessive hand on her thigh. "Besides, I think they're going to say, 'She's stunning. He's one lucky guy'. Or, 'She's a talented photographer. Is that her assistant? Maybe he's her muse'."

She shot him a grin. "You *are* my muse."

"And you're mine. I've become very inspired these past two weeks."

"And closed-lipped. You haven't said a word about Starry Cove. I can't wait to see what you've been up to."

"And I can't wait to show you."

She folded her hand over his.

Driving west, they chased the sun as it continued its afternoon descent. Forty minutes later, Zander exited the interstate and wove through the familiar country roads to surprise number one.

The Cove.

His heart hammered hard against his ribcage. He was returning to the scene of the crime, the place where it all began.

As he pulled into the abandoned drive-in movie theatre parking lot, Savannah said, "Wow." She shot him a grin. "You *have* been busy."

The place was swarming with construction workers. Three bulldozers worked to clear out the debris.

"Surprise, babe." With a smile, Zander exited his truck.

After getting out, she surveyed the area.

"If you want to head down there, I can grab hard hats," he said.

She clutched his hand. "I'm good here."

"I bought the land and I'm restoring The Cove to its original state, but with all of the modern tech." He pointed. "The drive-in movie screen will be over there. And the snack shack will be there. Star gazing happens after the movie."

She stroked his back. "This is awesome."

"What do you think about renaming it The Kyle King Cove?"

Facing him, her eyes grew moist. "I love it. But won't that be difficult for you?"

"Thinking back on my childhood will always be a struggle, but my dad led me to you, and for that, I'm grateful."

She choke-sobbed and turned away from him.

He pulled her into his arms, stroked her head. "Our first kiss was right here. That one, taboo kiss changed *everything*."

With a tender touch, he wiped away her tears before dropping several worshipful kisses on her lips. When she hugged him, he knew he'd made all the right choices.

Stepping back, she clasped his hands. "I love it, but what do the residents think?"

"Thumbs up all around. They've already created an arts committee and are planning a movie schedule."

"This is the best surprise."

"If you like this one, you'll *really* like the next one."

Her eyes grew wide. "There's more?"

They left The Cove and headed into town. Too many days had passed with only a virtual connection, so he blanketed her thigh with his hand. She responded by threading her fingers through his.

He drove onto Main Street and slowed to a crawl. "The inn is getting a complete overhaul. We can talk about the specifics later."

"Oh, I'm going to be busy *later*. Very, very busy. But I have time tomorrow morning, say, around eight?"

He shot her a grin. "I like the sound of that."

He parked in front of an abandoned two-story building across the street from the B&B. "I've got something to show you."

She stepped onto the sidewalk as he rounded the front of the vehicle. With his hand on the small of her back, he guided her to the storefront, unlocked the door, and ushered her inside. When she crossed the threshold and surveyed the spacious room, he held his breath. The empty space had been gutted, cleaned, and painted a bright white.

"This is a great location. Open, lots of windows, good vibe. What's going in here?"

"The Savannah Morrissette Art Gallery."

"Oh, my God." She spun around, her eyes glowing brightly. "Are you serious?"

"Do you like it?"

"I *love* it. It's amazing!"

He anchored his hands on her shoulders. Touching her felt so damned good. "I've been dying to tell you, but wanted your approval first. I'm purchasing the building in both our names. Once we're up and running, we can feature local artists to support their work, too, if that's something you want to do." Pausing, he studied her face. "Thoughts?"

She threw her arms around him and kissed him full-on. He wrapped her in his arms and lifted her off the ground.

When the kiss ended, he set her back down. "So, just to confirm, that's a yes, right?"

Again, tears welled in her eyes and she brushed away the ones tumbling down her cheeks. "I can't believe you did this...for me." With a gentle touch, she swatted his shoulder. "Look at me, I'm a mess. You've turned me into a crybaby, Zander King."

He chuffed out a laugh. "It's a lot to take in." Tipping her chin toward him, he brushed his lips to hers. "I did it because..." He swallowed hard. "Because I love you."

Her beautiful smile relieved him of any concern he had over expressing his feelings. "I love you, too," she said and kissed him. "There were times over the past two weeks when I wanted to tell you how I felt. I'm glad I waited. In person is much better."

He stared into her soulful eyes, dropped a tender kiss on her forehead. "I agree. And I've got one more surprise, if you can handle it."

"You're spoiling me, Zander."

He trailed his hand down her back. "I love making you happy."

She stilled. "That's the nicest thing anyone has ever said to me."

"We'll come back tomorrow after meeting with the contractor I hired for the inn. You two can discuss your ideas for this location, too. If you're interested, I have a few suggestions of my own."

"I welcome your input." She kissed his cheek. "Always."

The sun dipped below the horizon as Zander drove Savannah to his father's Victorian home in a well-established neighborhood, an easy ten-minute drive from Main Street. After pulling into the driveway, he gestured toward the home. "You want to go inside?"

"Sure."

Over the past two weeks, he'd been there twice. What had surprised him most was a framed picture on his father's desk. When Zander had been in second grade, he'd earned straight A's for the first time. His dad had snapped his picture with his report card. He'd lost both his front baby teeth, and his toothless grin filled his young face. He never knew his dad had saved that snapshot, let alone framed it. As Zander had walked through his dad's home, he made peace with his past.

Today, however, he was forging a path to his future, one he hoped included Savannah.

After getting out of the vehicle, she grabbed her carry-on bag.

"Let me get that for you," he said, taking the item. "Do you want your luggage, too?"

"That depends on what you have in mind, Mr. King." She waggled her brows. "Are we staying or just passing through?"

"Staying."

"Better grab it now."

He snagged a kiss before opening the hatch and pulling out her bag. They walked up the path and into the house. After setting down the bags, he flipped on the foyer lights, and closed the front door.

In one fluid move, he backed her against the old, wooden door, cradled her neck in one hand, and squeezed the back of her thigh with the other. Moaning into him, she grasped the lapel of his sport coat and pulled him closer. Their kiss was a heady mix of unfiltered desire and love. She melted into him and, when the kiss ended, she sighed.

"I'm so damn happy to see you," he murmured, stealing another kiss.

She palmed his crotch. "I can tell. Why don't we take this celebration to a more comfortable surface?" With a spark in her eyes, she nudged him back.

"The housekeeping service did a nuclear clean. Even so, I threw out the old bedding. New mattresses and linens on every bed in the house."

"You think of everything," she said.

"Mostly, I've been thinking about you."

Her sultry smile turned up the heat level. "Mmm, I like the sound of that. I vote to head upstairs *now* so you can show me those silky new bedsheets."

"You read my mind." He took her hand and led her to the second floor.

As soon as they entered the master suite, Zander pulled her into his arms. One tender kiss turned incendiary, and they tightened their hold on each other. While kissing her, he began unbuttoning her shirt while she unbuckled his belt.

Gasping for breath, she broke away. "Strip. Now."

"You, first. And I'll do it."

He curled his hand around her wrist and unfastened the cuff button, then repeated the gesture on her other sleeve. Next, with his gaze fixed on hers, he undid her shirt, one agonizing button at a time, as if he had all the time in the world. When he finished, only her sexy black lace bra separated him from her beautiful breasts.

Her breathing shifted, her pupils dilated. She ran her tongue over her lips until they glistened. Her intoxicating scent drew him closer and he kissed her again.

While he was eager to get her naked and slide inside her, he loved pleasuring her just as much. He wanted her to squirm and pant from the pleasure he could bring her. Their numerous video chat sex sessions had been fun, but virtual eroticism wasn't his thing. Being with Savannah, in the flesh, was uncensored, unfiltered, and wild.

Yet, this time, he needed tender lovemaking, too. Now that he'd admitted his true feelings, he couldn't wait to show her how much he adored her.

He shouldered off her shirt, then paused to admire her pert breasts and erect nipples as they strained to escape her bra.

"Now, who's spoiling whom?" He dipped his head, kissed her nipples through the thin material. "So damned beautiful."

Her low moan sent adrenaline shooting through him. He loved arousing her, seeing her heavy lids, her parted lips, her breasts rising and falling with each jagged breath.

Next, he removed her heels and pants. With those gone, he slid his fingers along the edge of her black thong, dipping down to graze her clit.

"Zander," she whispered, the urgency in her voice a clear sign she was ready for him.

"Let's take our time, baby. I'm just starting to dote on you. All you have to do is relax and enjoy." He slid her thong down and kissed her. "You smell delicious."

"I want you in me." Her guttural command made his stiff dick ache.

"So greedy." He rose, shrugged out of his sport coat, yanked his sweater over his head. Then, he dropped his pants.

Her smile undid him. "Somebody didn't bother with underwear." She caressed his shaft. "Touching you feels good."

He slipped his fingers between her legs and stroked her sensitive folds. "You're dripping wet, Savannah."

"Uh-huh. I'm happy to see you." She slipped her free arm around his waist, dropping her hand on his ass. She stroked his skin, pressed her lips to his. "I want to ask you something."

He caressed her back, unhooked her bra, and pulled it off. "Anything."

"Did you always wear condoms with former partners?"

He ran his tongue over her nipple. "Always."

"I insisted on condoms, too. But I don't want us to use them now."

He closed his mouth around her nipple while he fondled her other breast. Raw heat surged through him. When he bit her nipple, she cried out.

"I love that. Do it again."

He bit her other one and she sunk her fingers into his hair. "So good."

He continued alternating breasts until her moans grew raspy and she dug her nails into his back. Then, he framed her face in his hands and kissed her. "Loving you is the easiest thing I've ever done and I want you to feel my love every day."

Her lips quirked on her flushed face. "I'd like to feel that love between my legs. Would that be possible in…say…the next *two* minutes?"

He whisked her into his arms and carried her to the king bed. In truth, he couldn't wait, either. As they lay together, her beauty and sensuality radiated. He dropped a light kiss on her lips. "What did you say about condoms?"

She pointed to her arm. "I use the birth control implant. I don't want to use a condom tonight. I want you. Just you in me. Nothing separating us. Skin against skin *everywhere*."

Zander King needed no convincing. "I'm clean."

"So am I, but I'm about to get dirty. Very dirty."

Jolts of energy shot through his ramped-up body.

She reached down, guided him to her. The slide inside exhilarated him. Her moans thrilled him. The pleasure overpowered him and he got lost in how good they were together. He had no concept of anything but Savannah, beneath him. Her fingers trailed over his back, through his hair. Every kiss, every stroke brought him closer to her.

He murmured his love for her and, when she smiled, he rolled them over, putting her in control. He trusted her with every ounce of his being. He could be vulnerable and unsure, brave and over-controlling. Every moment of his life had built to a climax with someone he'd once regarded as family.

Now, she wasn't just his business partner, she was his beginning. And if he loved and cherished her, she would be his middle and his ending, too.

She kissed him and began moving on him. He smiled, the joy and rapture rolling over him and through him. He opened his eyes, whispered her name. Her pace accelerated as she took him deeper and deeper inside her.

This free-spirited woman and their impassioned connection had been the missing piece in his life. He knew in his soul that she was the one. He'd first known when she refused to muss his hair at Petroglyph National Monument. He had no idea why that moment had affected him, but it had. Maybe because he'd realized then that she held the power…over his heart.

That random weekend had changed his life, *forever*.

Crying out his name, she shook and trembled, her body releasing a powerful orgasm that rocked him to his core. And he let go, the ecstasy binding his soul to hers.

He had sealed his love for her in the most intimate way possible. Moments ticked by while they caressed and kissed, relishing their newfound love.

"Contentment is underrated," he said, finally breaking the silence.

She lifted her head. The intensity that had been in her eyes had been replaced with peace.

"I love the way you love me," she whispered. "I still can't believe you bought a building to display my work."

He tucked his arm behind his head. "We'll make it official tomorrow by signing the deed."

Tears pricked her eyes and she kissed him. "It's overwhelming you love me that much."

"Love, adore, admire, respect."

"Zander, I will make you proud. I promise."

"You never have to prove yourself to me, Savannah. We're a team. If you can't trust family, then who can you trust?"

The spark in her eyes flickered.

"I'm sorry, honey," he said. "Bad analogy."

She stroked his shoulder. "Being intimate with you is more than having sex. It's about trust. Because of Debby, I have a hard time with that. K-Dad helped me some, but it's still a struggle."

"It'll happen organically, over time." He kissed her. "You'll see."

Her smile made him smile. "I love your confidence in us. It's very uplifting."

After showering together, she dressed in yoga pants and a comfortable shirt. He wore his black jeans and a T-shirt.

She handed him a gift bag. "A little something."

"Babe, you didn't have to do that." He pulled out a T-shirt covered with chili peppers and laughed. "It's hotter and spicier in New Mexico." After hugging her, he yanked off his black shirt and pulled on the new one. "It's awesome."

"You look great."

"I grabbed groceries at the store. How about a glass of champagne before I make you dinner?"

"I'd love one. But you have spoiled me enough. I'm making *you* dinner."

"We'll do it together."

Hand in hand, they strolled into the kitchen. While Zander pulled the bottle from the refrigerator, Savannah ran her fingers over the old oak table. "I miss K-Dad."

"I know you do. In my own way, I do, too."

As he popped the cork and poured the bubbly, she called out, "Forgot something upstairs. Be right back."

When she didn't return, he found her in the family room, staring at an array of framed black and white photos hanging on the wall. "For you." He handed her a flute.

"I took those shots in college," she said, accepting the glass.

Pausing, he admired the pictures of the snow-capped mountains. "Your work hangs in almost every room. It's like a mini Savannah Morrissette gallery."

"K-Dad was my biggest fan."

Zander gestured to the wrinkled brown leather sofa and she eased onto the corner cushion. "You doing okay here?" he asked, sitting beside her.

She draped her legs over his lap. "I've got you, so, I'm doing great. How do *you* feel about staying here?"

"I'm good." He clinked his glass against hers. "To us."

"To you, for making my dreams come true." After sipping the chilled drink, she took another. "This is delicious." Resting her elbow on the back of the sofa, she ran soft fingers through his hair.

Being with her, being touched by her, magnified his needs and soothed his heart at the same time. For a man who'd spent a lifetime blocking out the myriad of emotions swirling in his head, he welcomed the powerful affect Savannah had on him.

"It's one thing to live out a fantasy or have a fun weekend fling, but this—*us*—feels real…and right," he said.

"I'm blown away by everything you've done, but the one thing that matters to me is how much we care about each other." She set down the flute and captured his hand in both of hers, then kissed his knuckle. "I want you to be happy and successful. My agreeing to your plans for Starry Cove wasn't just the right thing to do for you professionally, it was the best thing to do for you personally, as well."

"Why's that?"

She hesitated, her gaze floating over his face. "Kyle didn't give you the love and acceptance you deserved. He didn't support your dreams. But I do."

His throat tightened and he bowed his head, embarrassed by the onslaught of emotion.

She cupped his chin, lifted his face to hers. "I don't want you to hold back with me, ever. I'm going to love you fully and completely."

He had no doubt. The love in Savannah's eyes shone brightly.

He drew her close and kissed her. "Being with you has changed my life. You've helped me slow down. I'm figuring out that there's more to life than working. Because of you, I'm learning how to be happy."

"I can see how happy you are." She handed him another gift, this one covered in tissue paper. "For you."

He unwrapped a framed picture of them at the Botanical Garden, the colorful blanket flowers in the background.

"This is a memory of one of the best days of my life," she said.

"You told me I made that day special, but you made it just as special for me. This is the day I started falling in love with you. I never want to lose the magic we captured that day."

He kissed her. "This gets hung in my office as a reminder of what's *really* important."

Love, tender and true, wove around his heart. "And since we're talking about what's important, Kent and I have had several conversations about our business."

"All good ones, I hope." She picked up her flute, sipped the chilled bubbly.

"Going forward, we're partnering with energy-efficient companies that focus on preserving as much of the natural environment as possible. We want to respect the land and build structures that honor its beauty, not detract from it. Turns out, we aren't the only ones concerned about this. We've already pitched two projects in that same vein."

She grinned. "I like that…a lot."

"I thought you might." He sipped the champagne. "We're committed to taking on more small-town projects and driving business back into the hands of local merchants. But the biggest change is that we're all about work-life balance. I scaled back from seventy hours a week to forty, and it feels like I'm working part-time."

"You *were* a workaholic."

"Those stress headaches were killing me."

"I love your plan and I'll do whatever I can to support you."

He clasped her hand, making small circles on her palm with his thumb. "I brought Kent and Megan here and they fell in love with the area. We're relocating King Development to Starry Cove."

Her eyes grew large. "That's huge."

"That's not all." His heart picked up speed. "This house is too big for me to live here alone."

"So, are you looking for a roommate?" Her playful expression made him smile.

"*No*, and I don't want a dog, either." Pausing, he studied her face. *This* was their defining moment. "I want to build a life with you, Savannah."

"Oh, Zander," she murmured.

"You can fly in and out of Dulles for your out-of-town gigs. Keep your beach home as our getaway place." Though confident in her love for him, he was unsure she'd be willing to make this drastic life change. *Ask her.* "Savannah, will you move in here with me? Turn this house into a home? *Our* home."

Love sprang from her eyes and she kissed him. "You don't have to sell me, babe. My answer is *absolutely* yes. I'd love to." She paused, her unwavering gaze making his heart pound hard and fast. "I can't imagine my life without you."

With a loving smile, she captured his face in her hands. He breathed her in and tightened his hold. His jitters floated away, replaced by a peace that settled his restless soul.

And when his lips melded with hers, he knew in his heart he'd come home.

EPILOGUE

May, twenty months later

S AVANNAH SHOOK THE WOMAN'S hand. "That's one of my favorite photographs."

"Mine, too," said the woman, "which is why I bought it."

Savannah laughed. "I hope you'll send me a picture when you hang it. I always love seeing where my work ends up."

"I love the Sandia Mountains."

"Me, too. I started falling in love with my husband while there on a location shoot. It's always a treat to photograph New Mexico's mountain ranges."

Megan Walker finished wrapping the framed photograph in brown paper. "Would you like me to put this in your car?"

"I've got this." The woman said her goodbyes and carried the package outside.

Megan closed the door to the art gallery and grinned. "My God, woman, you sold out."

"*We* sold out. This is a 'we' thing."

"What did I do?" Megan asked.

"What *didn't* you do? You alerted the press, you ran a fantastic

PR campaign, you arranged catering. And don't get me started about how amazing you are with our clients, especially the returning ones."

"You are so good for my ego, I can't stand it." Megan collected her handbag from behind the counter. "I hate to leave you—"

"Go. I'll clean up. What are you guys doing tonight?"

"Seriously, you have to ask me that?"

"Oh, right. Movie night at King Cove."

"Kent's grilling before we leave if you and Zander want to join us."

"Thanks. I'll text you after I talk with him."

"Just show up. And please know that if you don't come, Colin is going to be disappointed. I think he likes you two more than he likes Kent and me."

The women laughed.

Megan opened the gallery door and Zander breezed in. "Perfect timing. Where are you going?" he asked Megan.

"Home. Kent texted that my parents are worn out from spending the afternoon with three 'rambunctious' children. Their words, not mine. Gotta run." Megan hurried down the sidewalk.

Zander closed the door and kissed his wife. "Hey, baby."

"Hello, my love. How was golf?"

"We had a great time. Kent and I closed the deal on the ninth hole. Our shots tanked after that, but we were too happy to care. The client insisted we lost on purpose."

She laughed. "Congratulations! Which one? The Lake Norman project or the one in the Catskills?"

"The lake." He glanced around the gallery. "Where are all the photographs?"

Savannah smiled. "We sold out."

Zander picked her up and spun her around. "Congratulations. That's awesome."

She kissed him. "Total team effort, but thank you."

He set her down. "You still have one more day left in the show. What will you do tomorrow?"

She fiddled with her diamond ear cuff. "I'll contact nearby artists and invite them to offer their pieces. If no one's available, I'll serve free food all day and mingle."

"Nice. Kent mentioned they're headed to The Cove for movie night. Do you want to join them?"

"I'm flexible. I have a little something for you."

"A present for me?" He wrapped his hand around her skirt-covered bottom. "Should I lock the front door?"

Chuckling, she walked into the back room, returning with a small wrapped gift.

"We just celebrated our anniversary," he said. "My birthday isn't until November. What's this for?"

"It's an 'I love my husband' gift." She handed it to him.

He opened the small rectangular box. Inside was a home pregnancy test. "Oh, wow, Savannah." He stared at the results.

"The result of our *extremely* fun first anniversary vacation in Santa Fe."

He threw his arms around her and hugged her, then he kissed her with such tenderness, tears pricked her eyes.

"Best present *ever*." He wiped the tears. "I love you, wife."

"Right back atcha, Slick."

With a heartwarming smile, he knelt. "Hey, little one. It's Daddy. I love you and Mommy so much. Your job is to grow. I cannot wait to meet you." After kissing her tummy, he rose. "We'll have to start thinking of names."

She laughed. "I think we've got some time, Zander."

"Right. What about a delivery class?"

"Deep breath, honey. Again, time is on our side."

He inhaled, exhaled. "Does anyone know?"

She shot him a little smile. "Just us three."

"I love the sound of that."

"So do I," she said, and kissed him again. Then, she collected her cell phone from behind the counter. "A picture to remember this special day."

As Zander snapped the selfie, he kissed his wife's cheek. "Every day with you is worth remembering."

Gazing into his eyes, she smiled. "I feel the exact same way."

A NOTE FROM STONI

Thank you so much for reading Zander and Savannah's love story! Writing this contemporary romance was a fun departure from my usual intense romantic suspense novels. I also loved putting Zander and Savannah in New Mexico. It was my childhood home and a part of the country I hold dear to my heart.

If I'm a new-to-you author, I invite you to check out my wildly successful Touch Series. These romantic suspense novels are packed with twists, emotion, a ton of heat, and a very heartfelt Happily Ever After. While they can be read as standalones, I recommend starting with THE MITUS TOUCH since characters appear across books.

In the mood for another contemporary romance instead? I highly recommend BEAUTIFUL DISASTER. Sparks fly when Jett St. John, a down-and-out Hollywood bad boy, meets Cassidy Clarke, a gorgeous image consultant. He desperately needs her help. She wants nothing to do with him…because of their past. What could possibly go wrong?

It's always fun to hear from readers. You can drop me a note at Contact@StoniAlexander.com.

To learn about my upcoming releases, be the first to see a cover reveal, or participate in a giveaway, sign up for my Inner Circle newsletter at StoniAlexander.com. When you do, I'll send you my steamy short story, MetroMan.

All of my books are available exclusively on Amazon and you can read them FREE with Kindle Unlimited.

Cheers to Romance!
Stoni

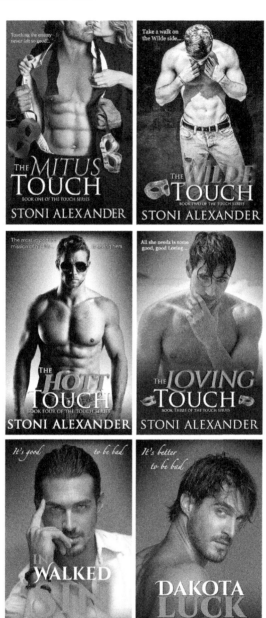

The Touch Series - Romantic Suspense

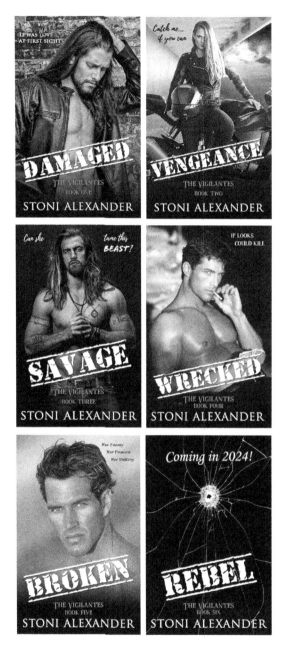

The Vigilantes Series - Romantic Suspense

Looking for a sexy standalone?

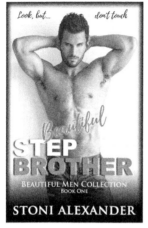 

Beautiful Men Collection - Contemporary Romance

Grab them or Read FREE with Kindle Unlimited!

ACKNOWLEDGMENTS

My heartfelt thanks to the following people who helped make **BEAUTIFUL STEPBROTHER** a better story.

Nicole, your edits are fantastic. This time, however, you provided invaluable feedback at the storyline level. Thank you so much.

Carole, I am forever grateful for your attention to detail. This time your proofreading skills went above and beyond. Thank you for catching that *faux pas*.

My critique group tells it like it is! Thank you Magda, Andy, and M.C.

My heartfelt appreciation to my fantastic ARC Team for your support and enthusiasm.

Johnny, I am a lucky girl to go through life with you by my side. Thank you for being my rock.

Last and most importantly…

To my wonderful readers: I am blessed beyond words that you take the time to read my novels. I am especially grateful when you drop me a note to share a kind word. Thank you so much!

ABOUT THE AUTHOR

Stoni Alexander writes sexy romantic suspense and contemporary romance about tortured alpha males and independent, strong-willed females. Her passion is creating love stories where the hero and heroine help each other through a crisis so that, in the end, they're equal partners in more ways than love alone. The heat level is high, the romance is forever, and the suspense keeps readers guessing until the very end.

Visit Stoni's website:
StoniAlexander.com

Sign up for Stoni's newsletter on her website and she'll gift you a free steamy short story, only available to her Inner Circle.

Here's where you can follow Stoni online. She looks forward to connecting with you!

a amazon.com/author/stonialexander
BB bookbub.com/authors/stoni-alexander
f facebook.com/StoniBooks
g goodreads.com/stonialexander
O instagram.com/stonialexander

Printed in Great Britain
by Amazon

42878424R00111